The truth
could
change
everything...

An Unexpected
Amish Harvest

CARRIE LIGHTE

LOVE INSPIRED
INSPIRATIONAL ROMANCE

Uplifting stories of faith, forgiveness and hope.

Fall in love with stories where faith helps guide you through life's challenges, and discover the promise of a new beginning.

AVAILABLE THIS MONTH

ISBN-13: 978-1-335-75873-6

50599

S EAN

AN UNEXPECTED
AMISH HARVEST
CARRIE LIGHTE

LOST AND
FOUND FAITH
LAUREL BLOUNT

THE COWBOY'S
AMISH HAVEN
PAMELA DESMOND
WRIGHT

CHASING HER
DREAM
JENNIFER
SLATTERY

A MOTHER'S
STRENGTH
ALLIE PLEITER

THE BULL
RIDER'S FRESH
START
HEIDI McCAHAN

LIATMIFCO921

"I'm sorry about what I said, Susannah.

"It just slipped out," Peter murmured quietly.

"It's okay. Sometimes I say things without really thinking them through."

It felt strange to be sitting with Susannah, with no one else on the other side of the table or in the room. It reminded Peter of when they'd sit by the creek in the summer, dangling their feet into the water and chatting. And instead of pushing the romantic memory from his mind, Peter deliberately indulged in it as he lingered over his pie.

Susannah didn't seem in any hurry to get up, either. "How is your *mamm*?"

"She's okay," Peter said. He abruptly stood. "I'd better get going or your *grossdaddi* won't let me take any more lunch breaks after this."

Susannah replied, "Don't worry, my step-grandmother would never let that happen." She caught Peter's eye. "And neither would I."

Peter was overcome with affection. *"Denki,"* he said and then forced himself to leave the house while his legs could still carry him.

Carrie Lighte lives in Massachusetts next door to a Mennonite farming family, and she frequently spots deer, foxes, fisher cats, coyotes and turkeys in her backyard. Having enjoyed traveling to several Amish communities in the eastern United States, she looks forward to visiting settlements in the western states and in Canada. When she's not reading, writing or researching, Carrie likes to hike, kayak, bake and play word games.

Visit the Author Profile page at Harlequin.com.

An Unexpected
Amish Harvest

Carrie Lighte

LOVE INSPIRED
INSPIRATIONAL ROMANCE

LOVE INSPIRED®
INSPIRATIONAL ROMANCE

Recycling programs
for this product may
not exist in your area.

ISBN-13: 978-1-335-75873-6

An Unexpected Amish Harvest

Copyright © 2021 by Carrie Lighte

This edition published by arrangement with Harlequin Books S.A.

For questions and comments about the quality of this book, please contact us at CustomerService@Harlequin.com.

Love Inspired
22 Adelaide St. West, 40th Floor
Toronto, Ontario M5H 4E3, Canada
www.Harlequin.com

Printed in U.S.A.

But he answered and said, It is written,
Man shall not live by bread alone, but by every
word that proceedeth out of the mouth of God.
—*Matthew* 4:4

To my faithful readers, with much gratitude

Chapter One

"**Y**ou're so thin!" Susannah Peachy's stepgrandmother, Lydia, exclaimed as they embraced each other. "I hardly recognize you."

It had been nine months since twenty-three-year-old Susannah had visited the small but growing Amish district in New Hope, Maine. At that time, she'd weighed about forty or forty-five pounds more than she did now, so her figure had been much rounder. Her face had been fuller, too. But she still had the same caramel-brown eyes, long, straight nose and thick brunette hair that was so curly that not even pulling it back into a bun could tame it. By the day's end, it always seemed to fluff up from her scalp, lifting her prayer *kapp* and making her appear slightly taller than she had in the morning. So it was a bit of an exaggeration for Lydia to say she hardly recognized Susannah, although she supposed it was a surprise for the older woman to see her so much thinner.

"I might look a bit different but I'm still the same person I was before," Susannah assured her. "Being thinner doesn't make me any different on the inside.

Kind of like wearing that cast on your arm doesn't make *you* any different."

"I wouldn't be too sure of that. Having this cast on my arm makes me a lot *grumpier*," Lydia confessed. "Not because I'm in pain, but because I want to accomplish more than I'm able to, which frustrates me. I feel so restless. When I get into that kind of mood, I have to stop and remind myself how blessed I am that I only fractured my wrist when I fell. I could have broken a hip! So I have nothing to complain about—especially since you've *kumme* to help me."

Susannah suspected there were a number of young women in New Hope who could have assisted her maternal grandfather's wife, but clearly Lydia preferred Susannah's company. Her grandfather, Marshall Sommer, had always doted on his only granddaughter, too. And, of course, Susannah loved them both very much, as well. But if she'd had her way she wouldn't have come to visit her grandparents in Maine. Instead, they would have returned to Dover, Delaware, to visit Susannah and her father, along with her brother and his family.

However, when Lydia broke her wrist and asked Susannah to come and keep house and cook for the farm crew during harvest season, she couldn't say no. It would have been unthinkable to refuse to help a family member in need, especially since her grandparents were getting up there in age. Only the Lord knew how many more opportunities Susannah would have to spend time with them.

Besides, it wasn't as if she was going to be overwhelmed with work. The crew consisted of only four men; two were local and the other two were Lydia's fourteen-year-old twin great-nephews, Conrad and Jacob, who were coming from Ohio. Which meant Susannah would actually be cooking and keeping house for fewer people here than she usually helped her sister-in-law cook for back in Delaware. So in a way, coming to her grandparents' farm might feel like a holiday visit by comparison. Especially since Susannah shared her grandparents' fondness for Maine.

Yet she was already counting the days until she could go home. Today was Friday and the crew was scheduled to begin harvesting on Monday. They'd spend three or four weeks picking potatoes, depending on how often it rained during that time. That meant at a minimum, she'd see her former suitor, Peter Lambright, at least two or three times in church, which met every other week. But as far as she was concerned, that was two or three times too many.

"You must be *hungerich* after being on the road since the wee hours of the morning," Lydia said, interrupting her thoughts. "I made a peanut-butter pie. I had to hide it in the fridge behind the lettuce so your *groossdaadi* wouldn't see it and ask me for a piece before you arrived. Let's have a slice with tea before supper. You can fill me in on all the news from Dover."

Susannah hesitated. "*Denki*, but I'm not *hungerich*. I'll wait until supper to eat, but I'll have tea with you."

Lydia lowered her silver, wire-framed glasses and peered at Susannah. "But I thought peanut-butter pie was your favorite? That's why I made it. It might be a little lumpy because I had to mix it using my left hand, but I think you'll still enjoy it."

Susannah didn't want to explain that she'd gotten into the habit of only eating dessert once a week. Usually she ate it following a light meal, not in the late afternoon before she'd even had her supper. But she appreciated how much time and effort it must have taken for Lydia to make the pie with one arm in a cast. She figured this one time she could indulge in a taste…especially since she was serving it, so she could cut herself a little piece. "Your pie is always *appenditlich* and it was thoughtful of you to make it for me. I guess a smidgen wouldn't spoil my supper," she said. "If you go sit in the living room, I'll be right in with it."

After putting the kettle on the gas stove, Susannah removed the pie from behind the lettuce on the bottom shelf of the diesel-powered refrigerator. As soon as she saw the white creamy custard topped with a crumbly peanut-butter-and-powdered-sugar mixture, her mouth watered.

She set it on the countertop, remembering when she'd spent the summer in New Hope a year ago, Lydia would make a peanut-butter pie at least once a week because she knew it was Susannah's favorite. Lydia didn't like the pie nearly as much as Susannah and Marshall did, so the two of them would more or less split it over the course of a couple of days. The only other person who could make such a delicious peanut-butter pie was Susannah's mother, who had died four years ago.

Mamm *didn't take very* gut *care of her health*, she thought sadly. Neither had her father. That's why last winter Susannah had changed their diet. Her father was overweight, too, and he'd briefly been hospitalized for complications from his diabetes. The *Englisch* doctor indicated if he didn't get his blood sugar under control, he could suffer kidney, nerve or eye damage, or cardio-vascular problems.

At first, Susannah's efforts to help improve his health were met with resistance. Surprisingly, the pushback didn't come from her father; it came from her sister-in-law, Charity, who had remarked, "How can bread be unhealthy when I make it myself? It's not as if it's store-bought and full of preservatives. And the *Lord* made corn and potatoes, so they must be *gut* for us."

Susannah had shared what she'd learned about eating whole grains, nonstarchy vegetables and protein, as well as "good" fats and dairy. And all of it in moderation. But Charity continued to turn up her nose at the dishes Susannah prepared until she saw how the pounds seemed to slide right off her and her father's blood-sugar readings stabilized. Then Charity helped Susannah peruse cookbooks from the library for healthier meal ideas and recipes, too.

"I'm *hallich* to be losing weight because now I have more energy," Susannah had told her. "But I'm especially *hallich* that the *dokder* said if *Daed* keeps these habits up, he might be able to stop taking his medication."

Still, there were a few members of her church district who were worried about Susannah's weight loss. She'd been mildly overweight for most of her life, so some people initially assumed she was ill. Others expressed concern that she was focusing too much on external appearances, or was becoming *hochmut*. High-minded. Proud. Not merely about how slender she had become, but also about the knowledge she had gained, even though she never flaunted her weight loss or offered nutritional advice unless someone asked her for it. However, after the novelty wore off, they became accustomed to how she looked and what she ate or didn't eat for lunch after church or during other community events. And eventually they stopped making comments, much to Susannah's relief.

But it seemed she'd have to get used to hearing similar comments all over again, because as they were enjoying their sweet treat, Lydia remarked, "Wait until Dorcas sees you. She's going to be astonished at how *gut* you look."

Susannah pushed a big forkful of pie into her mouth so she wouldn't respond brusquely. Ideally, Amish people didn't place an undue importance on superficial appearances, which was the very reason some had been critical of her when she first started slimming down. Yet she frequently noticed that even though *she* was discouraged from focusing on her weight, other people had no qualms about drawing attention to it. Regardless of whether their comments were positive or negative, the fact that they made more than just a passing remark about it seemed hypocritical to her.

She attempted to redirect the conversation, as she'd become adept at doing. "I'm really looking forward to catching up with Dorcas in person again. Although we probably won't spend too much time together, since she'll be working at Millers' restaurant."

When Susannah stayed in New Hope last summer, she had quickly formed a close friendship with Dorcas Troyer. The two young, single women had enjoyed each other's company again when Susannah returned to New Hope for a week at Christmastime, and they'd written to each other frequently throughout the last year.

In fact, Dorcas was the only person that Susannah had confided in when Peter asked to be her suitor the previous summer…and the only person Susannah had told about their breakup last January. She still remembered teardrops splashing onto the stationery as she wrote,

> Peter wouldn't give me any reason for ending our courtship, other than to say he doesn't think we're compatible, after all. But I know it's because I've gained so much weight since last summer.

Her friend had written back,

> I've known Peter for years and I can't believe your weight is such an issue for him. Are you sure that's why he broke up with you? Could it be that he just finds it too difficult to carry on a long-distance courtship?

Susannah highly doubted that. After she'd left New Hope the first time, Peter's biweekly letters had been filled with proclamations of his affection for her. The couple had called each other at their respective phone shanties at three o'clock every other Sunday. Even after two hours of talking, they'd never run out of things to share and laugh about. And although they had only been able to sneak off for an hour with each other when Susannah came to New Hope last Christmas, they'd agreed their time alone together was the best part of the holiday.

That's why it was so confusing that four days after she got home, Peter called and said he had decided to end their courtship. The change in his attitude was so abrupt it made Susannah feel as if he was an utter stranger. As if someone else had been pretending to be him on the phone and in his letters. Had been pretending to fall in love with her the way she'd been falling in love with him.

"Why?" she had cried, as bewildered as she was devastated. "I don't understand."

"We're just not a *gut* match."

"But *why* aren't we a *gut* match? What has changed all of a sudden?"

"I'm sorry to hurt your feelings like this, Susannah, but I don't want to discuss it further. Please accept my decision."

Afterward, she went over it and over it in her mind, trying to figure out what could have possibly changed to make Peter end their relationship. The only thing she could come up with was that once he'd seen her again, he was no longer drawn to her because of how much heavier she'd gotten. Maybe that was why he'd held his tongue about his reason; he hadn't wanted to hurt her feelings by telling her the truth. But whether he said it aloud or not, she'd been crushed to discover that Peter valued how she *looked* more than who she *was*. That he was rejecting her because of her weight gain.

Likewise, in the following months she was disappointed when certain other men *accepted* her because of her appearance. During the past spring and summer, she'd had no fewer than four bachelors in Dover ask to court her. Susannah would have felt honored, if it hadn't been for the fact that they'd all known her for at least ten years and they'd never expressed an interest in her until she was slender. So it insulted her and reflected poorly on their priorities when they'd asked to walk out with her once she was thin.

Nor did she consider it a compliment just now when Lydia suggested, "Hopefully you and Dorcas will have a chance to go to a singing together. You look so pretty that I wouldn't be surprised if half a dozen young men ask to be your long-distance suitor before you return to Delaware."

If they did, I'd say no, Susannah thought. If there was one thing she had learned about men this past year, it was that their feelings for her fluctuated along with the needle on the bathroom scale. And she'd rather be single than be loved for her appearance.

Just thinking and talking about suitors and court-ships made Susannah anxious and she again avoided responding to Lydia's comment. "*Denki* for making the pie for me. It was *appenditlich*," she said.

"You're welcome, dear. But you hardly had a sliver. Are you sure you don't want another slice?"

Susannah glanced down at her empty plate and sud-denly she felt rather empty inside, too. "I suppose a little more wouldn't hurt. Just this once."

After Peter Lambright helped his brother, Hannes, load the picnic table into the *Englischer*'s truck, Hannes closed the tailgate.

"Wait a second—we haven't loaded the benches," Peter reminded him.

Hannes chuckled and reopened the gate. "I'm so used to making A-frame tables, I forgot the benches weren't attached to this one."

Peter waited until they'd put the benches in the truck and the customer drove away, then said, "You've got to pay closer attention to what you're doing, Hannes. If you can't be trusted to remember something as basic as giving the customer the furniture he paid for—"

He clapped his hand against his cheek. "Oh, *neh*—I forgot to collect payment from him."

"Hannes! You've got to be kidding me."

"Jah." He grinned. "Collecting payment is the first thing I do."

Peter wasn't in the mood for his brother's shenanigans. "Quit horsing around. I need to know I can count on you this next month."

Hannes's grin melted and he replied solemnly, "Of course you can count on me."

"Gut. Then get back to work. I'm going over to the *haus* to check on *Mamm* and then I'm going to pick up Eva from *schul."*

Peter began walking toward the house, which was located a couple of acres east of the workshop. Twelve years ago, when the Lambrights had moved from Illinois to New Hope, his father had deliberately built the workshop as far from the house as possible. He was starting up a business—making picnic tables, porch swings and other wooden lawn furniture—and he didn't want customers driving too close to his children.

Their father had always been overly cautious around *Englisch* vehicles. That's why it still baffled Peter that one fall evening five years ago, his father apparently had forgotten to light the required lantern that hung from the side of the carriage. Or else the flame had gone out. Either way, the man driving a lumber truck behind him hadn't seen the buggy until it was too late to stop and he collided with the carriage, killing Peter's father.

His family had been devastated, of course, especially Peter's mother, Dorothy. But she faithfully relied on the Lord for comfort and strength. With His help and the help of her community, she was able to shepherd her children through their bereavement. Eventually, joy returned to the Lambright household…until late last autumn.

That was when Dorothy first experienced a significantly low energy level and an even lower mood. When it got to the point that she was staying in bed until noon, she finally consulted a doctor. He didn't find any physical cause for the change in her emotions and activity level, and diagnosed her with moderate depression, which she found both embarrassing and confusing.

"But I don't *feel* depressed about anything, except that I don't have more energy," she'd said afterward, instructing her children not to tell anyone about her diagnosis. Instead of accepting the prescription the doctor offered, she experimented with natural supplements and herbal remedies, to little avail. Hoping fresh air might help, she made it her goal to stroll with Eva, then twelve, to school each morning. But that only exhausted and overwhelmed her all the more.

It wasn't long before her friends noticed that Dorothy was less active in the community, her house was unkempt and she was often either weepy or irritable. Concerned, they suggested she visit a doctor, which she didn't want to do again. Some people in their district implied she was unwell because of unconfessed sin in her life. No doubt they meant to be helpful, but they did her more harm than good.

"I keep asking *Gott* to examine my heart and show me my sinful ways, and I keep trying to change," Dorothy had cried to Peter one Sunday after the church leaders had visited their house. "But I just can't seem to pull myself out of this. I'm so ashamed. And so, so tired."

I can't believe she's felt like this for almost an en-

tire year, Peter thought as he walked up the porch steps and into the plain two-story home. He found his mother sitting in the rocking chair in the living room, a shawl wrapped around her shoulders and an unopened Bible resting on her lap. She rubbed her eyes as if she'd been sleeping. Or crying.

When he greeted her, she replied, "What are you doing home? Is it suppertime already?"

It wasn't—not that it would have mattered; his mother rarely made supper anymore. She rarely *ate* supper anymore, either. But it was hard to say whether that was because *she* had no appetite or because the meals thirteen-year-old Eva made from a box or a can were unappetizing.

"*Neh.* I just came to see if you need anything from the store. I'm going to go stop at the Sommers' *haus* on my way to pick Eva up from *schul*," he said. The school was close enough that his sister usually walked home, but he thought he'd surprise her by giving her a ride. "I need to ask Marshall if he needs me tomorrow or if we'll wait until *Muundaag.*"

"Needs you for what, *suh*?"

"I'm helping him with the harvest, remember?" Peter had told his mother several times that he was going to help Marshall Sommer harvest his potato crop this autumn. But when her cheeks reddened and her eyes brimmed with tears, Peter realized he must have sounded impatient. When she was especially tired, Dorothy couldn't concentrate and she was sensitive about her forgetfulness.

"Oh, that's right. But I still don't understand why you wouldn't send your *bruder* instead. Picking potatoes is something a *kin* could do."

She had a point—children much younger than Hannes did the potato picking on the weekends on New Hope's other potato farm, owned by the Wittmer family. And in the *Englisch* communities up north, students had a three-to-four-week break every autumn, so the high schoolers could help with the local harvest. Not just picking, either—he'd heard of sixteen-year-olds driving trucks with upward of 50,000 pounds of potatoes on them. But here in New Hope, potato farms were an anomaly. The Amish children didn't get a break from school to bring in the crop, although sometimes they helped out on the weekends. So there would be another man, someone from the nearby Serenity Ridge district, who also would be joining the crew.

"I'm going to do more than pick—I'll be transporting potatoes to the potato *haus*, too. There's a lot of heavy lifting involved, so I'm better suited for it than Hannes is." While it was true that his brother had a slighter frame, that wasn't actually why Peter was the one who was helping Marshall on the farm. But Peter couldn't tell his mother the *real* reason, since he and Marshall had agreed they wouldn't discuss the matter with anyone else.

She smiled wanly. "Well, it's very kind of you to give him a hand, especially without pay. You're like your *daed* was—a *gut* provider to your *familye* and a *gut* helper to your neighbor. You'll make a *wunderbaar* husband and *daed* one day, just as soon as you meet the right *weibsmensch*."

Helping Marshall has nothing to do with kindness, Peter thought as he guided his horse down the road a few minutes later. *And I'm not nearly the* mann *my* daed *was.* As for meeting the right woman, Peter had already met her: Susannah Peachy, Marshall's granddaughter...

A horn sounded behind him, startling Peter from his thoughts. Then the car accelerated and passed him on the narrow, curvy country road, a risky maneuver. He shuddered as he recollected his brother's behavior in an *Englisch* vehicle last New Year's Eve, when the seventeen-year-old had driven an SUV off the side of an icy hill, flipping it twice and landing it in a ravine.

Blessedly, Hannes had emerged from the wreckage with nothing more than a few bruises and a sore shoulder, but the vehicle had been rendered undrivable. Because the accident had happened on their private property, the owners—parents of an *Englisch* acquaintance Hannes hung out with during his *rumspringa*—had agreed not to involve the police. In exchange, they required immediate reimbursement for the cost of the expensive vehicle.

Peter had to withdraw all of their shop's savings from the bank. But he'd still come up a few thousand dollars short of paying for the SUV. And there hadn't been a dime left over for immediate household and business needs. Ordinarily, Peter would have sought advice and possibly financial help from the church leaders, but there hadn't been enough time, since many of them were still out of town, visiting their families for the holidays.

Besides, he knew they would have insisted on discussing the matter with his mother and that was shortly after she'd been diagnosed with depression. Peter had been concerned that she'd sink even lower if she found out about Hannes's accident, especially considering how her husband had died.

Desperate, Peter had known he was going to have

to ask someone for money. The Amish in their district virtually never borrowed from *Englisch* banks or creditors, except when making a big land purchase. Instead, they sought loans from other community members, who generally considered it a personal obligation and a demonstration of their faith to help district members who came to them in need. These loans were handled with the utmost discretion and they were always interest-free.

Peter had turned to the one person he knew was in town and who could afford to help him: Marshall Sommer. It was humbling to ask a nonfamily member for money, but Peter had been in a long-distance courtship with his granddaughter, Susannah, and he hoped to marry her one day. So he felt a kind of kinship with the older man.

Understandably, when Peter made his request Marshall asked why he needed a loan. "My—my *familye* has r-run into some unexpected expenses that need to be addressed immediately. Expenses our b-business profits won't cover," he'd stuttered nervously. While vague, his answer was also truthful.

Marshall must have assumed he meant their business was in the red, because he'd lectured, "I'm surprised you haven't saved enough to take care of your *familye's* basic needs when sales are down."

Peter had felt humiliated, but there was nothing he could say in his own defense without disclosing his brother's situation. And he was afraid if Marshall knew that part of the money was going to be used to recompense *Englischers* for the damage his brother did, he would have suggested Hannes suffer the consequences. As Marshall had continued to chastise him for not being a good steward of the resources the Lord had provided,

Peter's face grew hot. If it hadn't been a violation of the *Ordnung*, he would have rescinded his request and borrowed from a bank, instead.

"*Jah*, I'll give you the money you need," Marshall had finally agreed when he was done delivering his discourse. "But instead of repaying me in cash, there are two things I expect from you. First, I need you to help me harvest next fall, since Lydia's two *seh* can't *kumme* next year."

His proposal seemed a fair exchange of money for labor. Since the fall was a slow sales period for lawn furniture, Peter figured Hannes could mind the shop by himself. "*Jah*. I'll help with the potato harvest. What's the second condition?"

"I want you to break off your courtship with my *kinskind*."

Peter had been so stunned that just thinking about it now made his stomach cramp. He'd had no idea that Marshall knew about their courtship and even less of an idea why he'd want to interfere in it. His response was a single word. "Why?"

"Because a man who isn't responsible enough to manage a *gut* income like yours isn't a man I'd want my granddaughter to consider for a husband," Marshall had bluntly replied. When Peter didn't—when he *couldn't*—respond, the older man reiterated, "I don't want you to court Susannah. If I can't convince you to end the relationship, I'll do my best to convince *her* you're not right for each other. Given what I know now, I believe she'll agree with me."

He'd understood. Even if Peter refused the loan, Marshall was still going to tell Susannah how irresponsible he thought Peter was and then *she'd* end the relationship. So, Peter had thought he might as well take the money and end their courtship himself. Once again, he'd been speechless.

"Do you need a few days to think about it?" Marshall had asked.

I didn't have *a few days. I barely had* one *day. And there was no one else I could turn to,* Peter rationalized to himself for at least the hundredth time since the day he'd accepted the old man's offer. *Marshall had been determined to break up Susannah and me. So what* gut *would have* kumme *from jeopardizing my* bruder*'s future and my* mamm*'s health by refusing the loan?*

At least by accepting it, Peter had kept Hannes out of trouble with the police. And while Dorothy's health hadn't improved, it hadn't worsened, either.

Yet try as he might to justify it, Peter still felt guilty. Only in retrospect did he fully realize that asking for a loan didn't make him a poor match for Susannah; it was breaking her heart in exchange for money that made him unworthy of her love. Unworthy of *any* woman's love.

As he journeyed the final mile toward the farm, Peter thought, *Within a month, harvest season will be over.* He had no hope of putting his mistake out of his mind completely. But maybe, just maybe, once he'd fulfilled his obligation to Marshall, Peter would be able to stop thinking about the pained, bewildered tone in Susannah's voice the day he'd called her and ended their courtship without so much as a word of explanation.

Susannah felt so drowsy after the long trip—and her second slice of pie—that she was tempted to take an afternoon nap while Lydia was resting. But she knew what she really needed was a walk in the brisk autumn air. She had just retrieved a sweater from her suitcase when she heard a buggy coming up the lane. *Groossdaadi!* she thought.

She raced outside and hopped down the porch steps, running up behind the buggy that had stopped just shy of the barn behind the house. Since her grandfather apparently hadn't seen her, she decided to sneak up on him, the way she used to do as a young girl. She knew now that she'd never really scared him, but she loved it that he always pretended to jump back in surprise, first throwing his arms in the air and then wrapping them tightly around her.

"Boo!" she exclaimed, springing forward once he'd climbed out of the carriage.

But as soon as the man turned, she immediately realized her error; although he was tall and broad-shouldered, he looked nothing like her grandfather. This man had wavy brown hair beneath his straw hat, his eyes were gray-blue and there was a small bump on the bridge of his nose. This man was Peter Lambright, her ex-suitor. She nearly stumbled backward in surprise.

"Hello. I'm Peter Lambright. You must be Lydia's niece," he said, smiling. She used to love that smile; it could keep her warm for hours, but now it turned her insides to ice.

Clearly, because of her weight loss, he genuinely didn't recognize her; it wasn't just an expression, like Lydia had used. *You didn't see me for who I really was when I was heavy, so I guess I can't expect you to see me for who I am when I'm thin*, Susannah thought bitterly.

"Neh. I'm Marshall's *kinskind,* Susannah," she retorted sarcastically, as if they'd never met. She crossed

her arms and lifted her chin in the air, waiting for the realization to sink in. His mouth dropped open and he appeared dumbfounded, so she asked, "What are you doing here?"

"I—I… I'm helping Marshall harvest this year. I came to ask whether he needs me tomorrow or if we're going to begin on *Muundaag*."

Susannah felt a surge of dizziness. She couldn't believe her ears. "*You're* helping with the harvest?"

"*Jah*. He—he asked me last winter if I'd help out since Lydia's *seh* couldn't *kumme* here this year." Red-faced, Peter fiddled with the reins, since he hadn't hitched the horse yet. "How long are you visiting?"

Susannah didn't want to chat; she wanted to flee, but it was as if her shoes were pegged to the ground. "Until Lydia's wrist heals."

Peter wrinkled his forehead. "Her wrist?"

"She had a fall and she broke it. I'll be cooking meals and keeping *haus*."

"I'm very sorry to hear that," he said grimly.

"Pah!" Susannah sputtered. She suspected he meant he was sorry to hear Lydia had broken her wrist, but it came out as if he was sorry to hear that Susannah was going to be staying throughout the harvest season to do the cooking and housekeeping. And *no one* was sorrier about that than *she* was. "My *groossdaadi* isn't home, but Lydia did mention that harvesting is still scheduled to begin on *Muundaag*, unless it rains."

"Okay. I'll *kumme* back then," he replied, yet instead of leaving, he lingered a moment longer, as if he wanted to say something else. Or maybe he wanted *her* to say something else. But she had absolutely nothing more to say. She tapped her foot against the ground impatiently and he swiftly scrambled back into his buggy.

As his horse trotted away, Susannah felt like weeping. *I didn't know how I was going to see him every other* Sunndaag *in* kurrich *without getting upset*, she thought. *How am I going to handle knowing he's right here on the farm six days of the week?*

Chapter Two

Peter felt light-headed as the buggy sped away from the Sommer farm. He'd been completely taken aback when he'd heard a female voice shout and then a woman had leaped out at him. Susannah Peachy was the last person he'd expected to see, so his brain didn't immediately register her face. He'd nervously introduced himself before he'd gotten his wits about him. Of course, once she spoke and he looked into her eyes—those beautiful, unforgettable almond-shaped eyes—he'd realized his mistake.

She must think I'm baremlich, *acting as if our relationship meant so little to me that I can't even remember her*, he thought. Which couldn't have been further from the truth; their relationship had meant the world to him, despite how he'd ended it. But the shame he felt for breaking up with her and the shock of seeing her again had overwhelmed him and he was stunned speechless.

Considering the circumstances, Peter would have appreciated it if Marshall had let him know Susannah was going to be at the farm during harvest. That way, he could have been praying the Lord would help him know what to say to her. Instead, he'd added insult to injury by behaving like a complete *dummkopf.*

Maybe he didn't tell me because he's afraid that I won't keep my promise—that I'll try to resume my courtship with her again, Peter thought. *Knowing him, he's doing his best to keep as much distance as he can between Susannah and me. Including waiting until the last possible minute to tell me she's here on the farm.*

Apparently, Marshall hadn't informed Susannah that Peter would be helping with harvest, either. It was possible the old man was worried that if she knew he was going to be on the farm almost every day, she wouldn't have come to New Hope. And to be fair, Peter wouldn't have blamed her, not after the piteous way he'd ended their courtship.

Nor did he blame her for looking at him so disdainfully a few minutes ago. Well, maybe she wasn't disdainful. Maybe it was disappointment he'd seen in her eyes. Or maybe Peter was just reading that emotion into her expression because that's how *he* felt about his own behavior. Regardless, he was aware that it had to be much more difficult for her to see him than it was for him to see her. *She* was the wronged party; he was the one who had wronged her.

I'll have to try my best to stay out of her sight while she's here—for her sake, as well as for mine, he decided as he pulled into the yard of the one-room schoolhouse.

Whenever he picked up Eva, he tried to arrive at the very last minute before school was dismissed so he wouldn't have to make small talk with the parents of the other students. It wasn't that he was unfriendly; it was that they inevitably asked about his mother and it was wearisome trying to answer truthfully while still respecting her wishes to keep her health situation private.

Not half a minute after he stepped down from the carriage, the school door opened and a crush of young children scurried down the steps, followed in close succession by the older scholars, as Amish students were called. Eva was one of the last to come out and she was hugging a cardboard box to her chest. Peter waved to get her attention and when she lifted her blond head and spied him, she smiled and quickened her pace.

Once they were out on the road, he pointed to the box between them and joked, "Is that your homework?"

"*Neh.* It's the youngest scholars' spelling tests and math worksheets. The teacher asked me to correct them tonight."

It wasn't unusual for the older students to help the teacher with the younger students' assignments during class and to correct their papers after school, but Eva was always volunteering to take on even more responsibility. Peter suspected she hoped that sometime in the future she could replace New Hope's current teacher if she resigned to get married and start a family. Eva provided the teacher a valuable service and she genuinely enjoyed correcting papers, but in the next few weeks, Peter was going to need her help at home more than ever.

"It's *gut* that you're willing to assist your teacher, but don't forget, starting on *Muundaag,* I'll be working on the Sommers's potato *bauerei* in the evenings for the next four weeks," he said. "And Hannes may have to work late if he can't keep up with the orders, so I'll need you to keep *Mamm* company."

"I haven't forgotten. But *Mamm* usually goes to bed

a lot earlier than I do so I'll have plenty of time to help the teacher with her paperwork."

"Perhaps if you suggested doing an activity together—quilting or playing checkers—*Mamm* might stay up later."

"But whenever I ask her to do something like that, she says *neh*, she's too tired," Eva argued. "You've been right there in the same room—you've heard her yourself."

Usually his sister's tone wasn't so flippant and Peter reacted impatiently. "There's no need to get *schmaert* with me, Eva. I know *Mamm* usually says *neh*. But that doesn't mean you should give up trying. I'm counting on Hannes to take care of the shop and you to take care of *Mamm* and the *haus* while I'm away. Understand?"

Almost immediately, Eva's eyes brimmed with tears. "Don't *you* understand? I *have* been taking care of *Mamm* and the *haus*. And I'd love it if she wanted to do something with me after supper. Even if all we did was sit on the porch and talk. But she never does…" She dissolved into tears, so Peter directed the horse onto the wide sandy shoulder of the road and came to a stop.

First Mamm, *then Susannah and now Eva—I sure know how to say all the wrong things to* weibsmensch *today,* he thought. He put his hand on his sister's shoulder as she cried. It was unlike her to be so tearful and it made him realize how deeply his mother's illness was affecting her, too. She'd been doing her best to take over all of the household tasks at home, without ever grumbling. Nor had she ever complained that her mother no longer engaged in activities—or even in conversation—with her, but Peter recognized now how much it must have saddened her.

When she stopped weeping, he said, "I'm sorry that right now *Mamm* isn't able to do the things she used to do with you. And I do appreciate how much you've taken over in the *haus*. I should tell you that more often."

"I don't mind doing the cleaning and cooking myself. But I can't *talk* to myself, the way I used to talk to *Mamm*." Eva sniffed. "I know she's still in the same *haus*, but it feels like she's a million miles away. What's wrong with her, anyway? Do you think it's really that she's depressed?"

"I don't know," Peter answered honestly. "But the Lord is our Great Physician, so I keep asking Him to heal her."

"I do, too." Eva heaved a sigh. "And I ask Him to give me more patience because it feels like forever since *Mamm* was—was *Mamm*."

Peter winced to hear his little sister describe exactly how he felt about their mother, too. "I have an idea. Let me get through the harvest first, and then if *Mamm* still isn't her old self, I'll convince her to go to the *dokder* again."

"How are you going to do that? You've asked her to go to the *dokder* as many times as I've asked her to work on a quilt or play a board game with me. She always tells you *neh*, too."

Peter had no idea how he'd finally persuade his mother to make another doctor's appointment, but he'd have plenty of time to think about it on the farm. Picking potatoes could be as boring as it was backbreaking, so having a challenge to think about would keep his mind occupied. "Leave that to me—and meanwhile, keep praying, okay?" Eva nodded but she still looked so forlorn that he suggested they should pick up a pizza for supper. "This way, you won't have to cook and you can grade those papers. I'll visit with *Mamm*, if she's up to it. And Hannes can take care of the animals."

"That would be great. Let's get the kind with ham and pineapple," she suggested, visibly perking up.

Relieved he'd finally made *one* female smile that day, Peter instructed the horse to giddyap. Unfortunately, he had a feeling it was going to take a lot more than a Hawaiian pizza to keep a smile on his mother's face. And as for making Susannah grin? Peter figured there was virtually no chance of that happening. *But at least if I avoid her, I won't make her frown*, he thought.

Susannah's meal was so salty she couldn't seem to drink enough water to quench her thirst. She and her grandparents were eating supper at a picnic table outside an *Englisch* diner in town because Lydia had insisted Susannah shouldn't have to cook her first night there. Susannah thought that was silly, since cooking was such a routine part of her life and she actually found it relaxing.

But then Lydia whispered that she wanted an excuse to get an extrathick milkshake before the restaurant closed on September 30 until Memorial Day of the following year. So Susannah had played along, telling her grandfather that yes, she really would enjoy eating out. And she would have enjoyed it, too, if everything on the menu wasn't fried or previously frozen. But since she didn't want to seem ungrateful, she ordered a burger with coleslaw instead of fries.

"I didn't realize Peter Lambright was one of the *menner* helping you with the harvest this season," she remarked to her grandfather in what she hoped was a casual voice. She had never told her grandparents about her courtship with Peter before and she certainly didn't intend to let on about it now.

Marshall finished chewing a large bite of fried chicken before replying. "How did you find that out?"

"He stopped by to make sure you didn't want him to start work tomorrow instead of *Muundaag.*"

"Hmpf." For some reason, he seemed disgruntled. "Since Lydia's two *seh* couldn't *kumme* this autumn, I had to recruit two other *menner* to help. Peter Lambright is one of them."

"Peter is a *wunderbaar* young *mann.*" Lydia's straw made a loud slurping sound as she finished the last of her milkshake. She set the empty paper cup on the tray. "Once he sees you again, I wouldn't be surprised if he asks to be your suitor."

Embarrassed that Lydia was discussing such a topic in front of her grandfather, Susannah looked down at her plate and picked at her coleslaw with a plastic fork.

"Don't be *lecherich.* She didn't *kumme* here to find a suitor." Marshall's gruff reply to his wife surprised Susannah. "She came to help *us.*"

Lydia persisted, "But there's no reason she can't help us *and* find a suitor, is there?"

Jah, there is a reason. A very gut *reason,* Susannah thought. *And that's that I'm not interested in a suitor and I'm* especially *not interested in Peter.* Susannah didn't answer aloud and neither did Marshall, but he hastily collected their used paper plates and cups and carried them on the tray to the recycling station.

"Your *groossdaadi* is so protective of you," Lydia whispered. "I don't know if it's because you remind him so much of your *mamm* or if it's because he doesn't realize that you're no longer a young *maedel*."

The comment was almost amusing coming from Lydia, since she also had a tendency to fuss over Susannah as if she wasn't a grown woman. "It's okay. He's right—I didn't *kumme* here to find a suitor." Susannah tried to sound as resolute as her grandfather had sounded, but she couldn't seem to get through to Lydia.

"If you're not interested in Peter, the other young *mann* who's coming from Serenity Ridge is a bachelor, too. Benuel Heiser. He's the one who's picking up the *buwe* at the bus station."

Susannah thought the other crew member was local, not from Serenity Ridge, so she was surprised to hear Lydia mention there would be an extra horse on the farm. "Benuel's staying at the *haus*?"

"Of course not—your *groossdaadi* would never allow that, not with you here!" Lydia exclaimed. "He's staying with his relatives just down the road. My greatnephews, Jacob and Conrad, will be the only ones staying with us…which reminds me, I didn't make up their beds yet. You'll have to do that for me. Now, do you have room for dessert?"

This time, Susannah didn't give in. "*Denki*, but I'm so full my stomach hurts."

Hours later, as she was lying in bed, her stomach *still* hurt. Whether that was from the amount or type of food she'd eaten that afternoon, or because talking about and seeing Peter had upset her, Susannah couldn't be sure. But she knew if she continued eating and feeling like she had today, she'd regret it physically and emotionally. So before falling asleep, she resolved she'd start the next day with prayer and an early morning walk.

Unfortunately, she overslept and was woken the next morning by the smell of sausages frying. She got dressed and hurried into the kitchen. Lydia was standing in front of the oven, where two large cast-iron pans were sizzling on the stovetop.

"How did you ever manage to lift those singlehandedly? I'm sorry I slept in—you should have woken me." Susannah looked into the pans. One contained thick slabs of ham and several sausages; eight eggs were frying in the other. Seeing the amount of food, she asked, "Did Jacob and Conrad get here already?"

Lydia looked confused. She backed away and sat down at the table so Susannah could finish preparing the meal. "*Neh*. They aren't coming until suppertime. Why?"

Susannah didn't want to point out that the breakfast was enough to feed half a dozen people, instead of just the three of them. It would have come across as self-righteous, considering it wasn't that long ago when she wouldn't have blinked at eating a breakfast this size. So she said, "I just want to be sure to make their beds up before they arrive."

After Marshall came in from the barn and they'd eaten their breakfast, Susannah washed and dried the dishes and then carried a stack of sheets and quilts to the open, unfinished loft upstairs. The beds weren't actual beds; they were borrowed mattresses lying on the floor. But after Susannah made them up, swept away the dust and washed the windows to a shine, she surveyed the room and thought, *It looks really cozy and comfortable up here. Especially for two scrappy fourteen-year-old* buwe *like Jacob and Conrad.*

She'd met the twins when she'd come to New Hope

the previous summer, and at the time, they'd been just about her height, so when they arrived shortly before supper, she was surprised to see they were now taller than her grandfather. And they were taller than Benuel, the sinewy auburn-haired man from Serenity Ridge who'd given them a ride from the bus station.

"You've really grown!" Susannah remarked as they all crowded into the kitchen.

"Jah," Conrad acknowledged with a lopsided grin. "And you've really shrunk!"

She supposed she had invited his remark and she would have dismissed it lightly, considering the last time they were together she and the twins had taken to teasing each other good-naturedly, like siblings sometimes did.

But then Jacob clarified, for Benuel's benefit, "He means she's lost a *ton* of weight. Last summer Susannah was twice as wide as she is now."

Although he said it admiringly, Susannah's cheeks burned. She didn't know how to respond without drawing more attention to herself. Just when she thought she couldn't feel any more embarrassed, Benuel came to her defense when he said, "I doubt that's true. I can't imagine her being that overweight."

"It's true. She was really—" Jacob began, but Marshall cut him off.

"Let's clear out of the kitchen so the *weibsmensch* can finish making supper. *Buwe, kumme* wait on the porch with me."

"Benuel, you'll stay for supper, too?" Lydia asked, but it wasn't really a question. When she invited someone to stay for a meal, she didn't take no for an answer. In this case, Benuel didn't need any convincing.

"Denki." He looked directly at Susannah as he added, "It smells *appenditlich.*"

The second the door closed behind them, Lydia whispered, "He seems like a nice young *mann,* don't you think?"

"Jah," Susannah replied distractedly, taking a stack of plates from the cupboard.

"And strong, too," Lydia insisted.

Aha. Now that she realized what Lydia was getting at, Susannah answered more cautiously, lest her own words be used against her. "That would explain why *groossdaadi* requested his help."

"I noticed *you* caught his eye." Lydia's silvery voice was too loud for Susannah's comfort.

She set the plates on the table, turned toward the oven and said, "I'd better stop gabbing and concentrate on finishing supper or I'll overcook this."

"What is it you're making?"

"Roasted vegetable casserole."

"That sounds *gut.* What kind of meat are you serving with it?"

"I didn't prepare meat. This is a very filling dish on its own."

"You're not going to win any *mann* over with nothing more than squash and brussels sprouts for supper," Lydia warned.

Her stepgrandmother's insistence that she should be trying to win a man over—winning him over with food, no less—was so exasperating that Susannah felt like screaming. But after a quick, silent prayer for grace, she was able to make light of the situation. She teased, "Then maybe I'll win him over with what I made for dessert."

Lydia narrowed her eyes. "I thought you said you didn't make dessert today."

Susannah snapped her fingers. "That's right, I didn't. Oh, well."

She giggled but Lydia just shook her head sadly, as if she didn't know what to make of a young woman who claimed little interest in having dessert and even less interest in having a suitor.

On Sunday morning, it took Dorothy so long to get ready for church that Peter considered suggesting she ought to stay home. But unless someone was out of town, in the hospital or seriously ill, an Amish person rarely missed church. Besides, Peter didn't want to discourage her, knowing she was doing the best she could to honor the Sabbath by gathering with others for worship. Still, by the time she got out the door, they were already late, and it was almost as much of a rarity for an Amish person to be tardy to church as it was to be absent from it.

Like the other settlements in that part of Maine, the New Hope district had constructed a building for their services instead of taking turns meeting in each other's houses, the way most Amish districts did. As the Lambrights approached the church, Peter felt self-conscious, knowing its large windows meant that everyone could see them. But at least the congregation was still singing hymns when his family tiptoed in, so they didn't disrupt the actual sermon.

The benches in the back of the room were filled, so Peter's family had to make their way to an empty bench halfway up the aisle. In their church, instead of the men and women sitting separately, as they did in some of the more conservative Amish churches, the families sat together. So once they took their places, Peter noticed Marshall and Lydia were occupying the bench two rows up from them. Two tall young men—presumably Lydia's nephews—were seated on the other side of Lydia, and Susannah was on the other side of the boys. To her right was a man Peter had never seen before; he would have remembered, as no man in their district had hair that color.

Did someone kumme *with her from Dover?* he wondered. *Her* bruder, *maybe?* But Susannah's brother was married with children; he wouldn't have come without them. Peter scanned the front half of the room but he didn't see any children he didn't recognize.

Then he caught sight of the Heiser family seated one row up from where Susannah was. Didn't Marshall mention that the crew member—Benuel, a bachelor Peter's age—was related to them? Peter deduced that there must not have been enough room for him on their bench, so he'd had to move back a row, joining Susannah and her relatives.

He tried to focus on the sermon, but Peter felt himself growing increasingly agitated to see Benuel and Susannah seated side by side. He wasn't troubled because it seemed as if they were a couple or because Peter himself wanted to be sitting next to her. He was troubled because he *used* to want to be sitting next to her. His favorite daydream used to be of the two of them going to church as husband and wife, and eventually filling a bench with their children. Seeing Susannah beside a man his own age made Peter keenly aware that he'd proved himself unworthy of being a husband and father by hurting the woman he loved in order to fulfill his own needs.

He sighed heavily, which startled his mother, who had fallen asleep against his shoulder. Dorothy jerked awake with an audible snort and Marshall glanced over his shoulder at her and scowled. Although it wasn't unusual for people to fall asleep during the three-hour Sunday sermon, usually those who dozed off were either teenage boys who'd been out late the evening before or elderly men. Dorothy covered her mouth with her hand, obviously embarrassed. And although he knew his mother really couldn't help falling asleep, at that moment, Peter was embarrassed by her drowsiness, too. He just wished he could disappear.

So when the service was over and Dorothy said she didn't think she could stay awake through lunch, Peter readily agreed they should go home, even though leaving church early was considered nearly as rude as coming to church late.

It was Marshall's turn to care for everyone's horses, so Susannah was relieved when he took Benuel, Jacob and Conrad outside with him. She'd felt self-conscious about Benuel's presence beside her throughout the worship service; single men and women virtually never sat together at church, even if they were courting, which they most definitely were not. However, no one else knew that and she was concerned people might jump to conclusions.

"I'll be more of a hindrance than a help in the kitchen," Lydia said as the women in the congregation began streaming downstairs to make lunch and the men stacked the benches atop of one another, transforming them into tables. "I'm going to go talk to the deacon's wife, Almeda Stoll, over there by the window. You'll be okay without me?"

"Of course." Susannah wasn't shy about pitching in. Besides, it would be nice to have a moment to catch up with Dorcas in private, if she could find her. She was so intent on scanning the room for her friend that she nearly bumped right into Eva Lambright, Peter's little sister, who was bending over to tie her shoe.

The summer Susannah came to New Hope, she and Lydia spent many afternoons picking wild blueberries with Eva and Dorothy Lambright in the field behind their house. She had treasured getting to know her suitor's family better, even though they were unaware she and Peter were courting. Despite how she felt about Eva's brother now, Susannah still had a soft spot in her heart for the girl.

"Oops. I'm so sorry. I didn't see you there, Eva," she said.

"Susannah? Susannah Peachy?" the young girl asked. Susannah braced herself for the inevitable comment about how much weight she'd lost, but instead, Eva excitedly called to her brother, "Peter, look who's back. You remember Susannah, don't you?"

That's when Susannah noticed Peter a few yards in front of them. He must have been trying to slink off without having to talk to her, because when he turned around, his face was red. Susannah used to love teasing him with sweet nothings and compliments until he blushed like that, but she certainly didn't feel like complimenting him now. *Please,* Gott, *help me to let go of my anger.*

"Hello, Susannah."

"Hello, Peter."

Their terse greetings were so stilted that Susannah was sure Eva would notice, but the girl seemed oblivious to their discomfort and continued chattering away. "I can't believe it's you. I was thinking about you this summer during *blohbier* season, but I didn't expect you'd *kumme* back to New Hope until *Grischtdaag*."

The young girl's fondness toward Susannah was evident and she couldn't help but smile back at her. "I came here to help Lydia cook and clean during harvest season."

"Really? What a coincidence—Peter's going to be helping your *groossdaadi* with the harvest. It's too bad I have to go to *schul*, or I could help, too. I really enjoy picking *blohbier*, but I've never picked potatoes before."

As his sister prattled on, Peter shifted his weight, inching toward the door. "*Mamm* and Hannes are probably done using the restrooms now and are waiting at the buggy."

"It's too bad we have to leave. It would be so much *schpass* to catch up with Susannah," Eva said wistfully. "I heard there are pumpkin bars with cream-cheese frosting and apple crisp for dessert. We don't have any homemade sweets at the *haus*. Ever since *Mamm* stopped—"

"Eva!" Peter interrupted, as if he was trying to silence her from saying something embarrassing. "We have more than enough food to satisfy your appetite."

A blush rose across Eva's chubby cheeks and she looked down at the floor. Susannah understood from personal experience how humiliating it was to have someone else make a comment, directly or indirectly, about a woman's appetite or weight. She was so irritated at Peter for implying his sister needed to cut down that she offered, "If you'd like to stay for lunch, my *groossdaadi* could give you a ride home, Eva."

Meeting Susannah's eyes again, Eva said, "*Denki*, but I have to go… Maybe you could *kumme* over to our *haus* for lunch next *Sunndaag*?"

Susannah caught her breath. *That's what happens if I speak when I'm angry—I make a bigger mess of things*, she thought, racking her brain for a gentle way to decline the invitation.

Before she could come up with anything, Peter supplied an excuse for her, obviously as opposed to the idea of her visiting his house as she was. "Susannah's grandparents might have made plans to bring her on visits with them next *Sunndaag*."

"*Jah*," Susannah agreed. "I'm afraid I don't know what my schedule is like yet. *Denki* for the invitation, though. I'm sure our paths will cross again eventually. Meanwhile, please greet your *mamm* for me."

"Okay, but if you find out you have a free afternoon or evening, you're *wilkom* to join us for lunch or supper anytime."

As Susannah watched the brother and sister leaving the room together, she thought, *Eva is such a* schmaert, *sweet* maedel, *but I'd rather go* hungerich *than to have to eat at the same table with Peter.*

Chapter Three

On Monday morning, after Peter finished his third helping of oatmeal, Hannes joked, "Do you want to lick the pot clean, too?"

"Harvesting potatoes is going to make me a lot hungrier than working in the shop is going to make *you*," Peter replied pointedly. "Would you like to switch places?"

"*Neh.* I'm *hallich* you're the one helping Marshall instead of me." Hannes looked him in the eye and Peter knew his brother really valued the sacrifice he was making on his behalf.

Getting extra hungerich *because I'm working outside all day is the least of what my* bruder*'s antics have cost me.* As soon as the bitter thought popped into his mind, Peter dismissed it. While he *did* want his brother to appreciate the consequences of his actions so he wouldn't repeat them, he didn't want Hannes to feel indebted to him.

For one thing, making a sacrifice for his family was part of Peter's duty as the head of his household. For another, Hannes didn't know Peter had broken off a courtship in order to pay for the car he wrecked. So Peter couldn't really blame him for that; he couldn't even blame Marshall. *I'm the only one at fault, because I agreed to it*, he thought.

"For lunch, I've packed you a couple of ham-and-cheese sandwiches, a container of broccoli salad and an apple," Eva announced, handing him a cooler. "I put several of those chocolate chip *kuche* in there, too."

Unfortunately, the cookies she was referring to were the kind that were wrapped in a plastic package and sold at the *Englisch* grocery store. Yesterday in church, Eva was being honest when she'd started to tell Susannah that they rarely had any homemade sweets in the house. Even though the meals Peter's sister put together usually didn't require much preparation time, going to school, keeping house, doing laundry and correcting papers kept her far too busy to make desserts. So she'd made a practice of buying cookies and cakes instead. Peter thought most of them tasted like cardboard coated in lard and sprinkled with sugar, and he rarely ate them, but today he'd likely be ravenous enough to eat almost anything.

"*Denki*. Please save something from supper for me, too, okay?"

"Are you sure you don't want us to wait to eat until you get home?"

"*Jah*. Sunset is around six thirty tonight and we'll have to make a final run to the potato *haus*, so I won't be home before seven. Maybe not even 'til eight."

Although Marshall was selling the potatoes to an *Englisch* buyer, he wouldn't allow *Englisch* technology on his property, including windrowers, tractors and trucks. So he'd be unearthing the potatoes with a horse-drawn mechanical digger. The crew would be "picking" them from the dirt and putting them in what they referred to as barrels, which were really cylindrical wooden containers that could hold sixty pounds of potatoes, since full barrels would have been too heavy for the men to lift.

After the crew had filled enough barrels, Peter and Benuel would load them onto the buggy wagon, which was a buggy designed specifically for hauling cargo instead of passengers. Then they'd take them to the *Englisch*-owned potato house, or storage building, for the *Englisch* buyer to transport them to the marketplace from there. The men would work in the fields from shortly after sunrise at six thirty until shortly after the sun set twelve hours later.

"That's going to be a long day. Maybe I should pack another sandwich to hold you over until you return?" Eva offered.

"*Neh*, that's okay. I've got to get going." Peter didn't want to reinforce Marshall's belief that he was irresponsible by showing up late to work. He reminded Hannes to check in on their mother a couple of times during the day, wished Eva a good day at school and then headed out the door.

I hope Mamm *is more rested today*, he fretted as he traveled toward the farm. Then his thoughts wandered to Susannah again. His second interaction with her had gone only marginally better than his first. He had tried to exit the church building surreptitiously so he wouldn't have to speak to her, but there had been no way to avoid it once Eva drew him into the conversation. And, in a way, it was a good thing she'd included him—otherwise his sister might have blurted out that their mother had been too tired or depressed to do any baking recently.

While Susannah had never been one to judge, Peter didn't want her to find out Dorothy had been struggling with fatigue this past year. Not only because it would have embarrassed his mother, but also because Susannah might mention it to her grandparents. *Marshall already holds a low opinion of* me—*I don't want him to decide* Mamm *is lazy, too. Especially because he noticed her sleeping in* kurrich *yesterday*, he thought.

So last evening, he'd gently reminded his sister that it was important not to discuss their mother's condition with anyone else. Eva had felt terrible for almost letting it slip in front of Susannah. "I'm such a *bobbelmoul!*" she'd lamented, explaining that she'd been so excited to see Susannah again that she'd rambled on without thinking. "I shouldn't have invited her over to the *haus*, either, just in case *Mamm* is having one of her really bad days."

"Don't worry," Peter had assured her. "It sounded as if Susannah's going to be too busy helping Lydia to *kumme* over here."

Even if Susannah didn't have a full schedule, Peter knew there was virtually no chance she'd be dropping in at their house. She may have invited Eva to stay and have lunch after church with her, but everything about her stance and tone toward Peter indicated she wanted to keep as much distance between the two of them as possible…just as he'd suspected.

As he neared the farm, his stomach tightened with apprehension and he silently prayed, *Lord, please bless my work in the fields and please keep me from seeing Susannah today. But if I do, please help me not to say anything to upset her.*

* * *

Susannah poured all of her frustration into scrubbing the greasy residue from a frying pan. On Saturday, after carefully preparing a menu, she'd gone shopping and bought enough groceries to last for three days, which was about all that would fit in her grandparents' small refrigerator. This morning's breakfast was supposed to include omelets, fresh fruit and yogurt with granola and a drizzle of honey. However, when Lydia learned what she was making, she insisted Susannah add pancakes and bacon to the meal, as well.

"Marshall and the *buwe* need more sustenance than that to keep them going until lunchtime," she'd insisted. "And we rarely eat yogurt, but when we do, it's the kind with fruit in the bottom, not that diet kind."

Since she felt it wasn't her place to object, Susannah had complied with Lydia's wishes. But inwardly, she'd argued, *It's not* diet *yogurt—it's plain. And the* buwe *will get plenty of sustenance from the protein in the* oier, *but I'm concerned about* Groossdaadi *having bacon—there's too much salt in it.*

While she was aware her stepgrandmother had only asked for her help cooking, not for her dietary input, Susannah's understanding of nutrition influenced what she made. Primarily because she cared about her grandparents and she had seen the effects of poor nutrition on her parents' health. Marshall and Lydia weren't overweight, but Lydia had mentioned Susannah's grandfather had high blood pressure.

Plus, Susannah had purchased groceries according to the menu she had planned. If her grandfather was going to expect to eat bacon every day, she'd have to go back to the store because Susannah had used up the last of what was in the fridge. *I can see if the store stocks reduced-sodium bacon. And at least the* buwe *will eat anything, so the food I already bought won't go to waste*, she thought.

After cleaning up the breakfast dishes, doing the laundry and sweeping the floors, she went into the living room, where Lydia was reading the Bible, and asked if she wanted to take a walk with her.

"A walk? Where do you want to go?"

"Just to the tree line out back," she suggested. Her grandparents' house was positioned on the western end of the farm, with the fields stretching to the east and north. Susannah figured if she walked across the grassy, unplowed meadow directly behind the house toward the tall pine trees, she wouldn't run the risk of bumping into the crew as they were harvesting the russets in the acreage closest to the house. More specifically, she wouldn't come within shouting distance of Peter.

"Why would we want to do that?"

Susannah anticipated the negative response she'd get if she told Lydia she wanted to walk simply because it was good exercise. Many of the Amish people she knew, especially those who were older, considered exercising for the purpose of exercising to be an *Englisch* pursuit. Physical exercise was a *result* of their lifestyle and hard work, but it wasn't considered the *goal*. So she carefully answered, "Because it's a pleasant way to enjoy the beautiful scenery *Gott* made. I don't get to see so many pine trees like this in Dover."

"That's why the windows are made of glass," Lydia teased. "Besides, it's a little chilly today. *Kumme* keep me company while I have another cup of *kaffi*. We haven't had a moment to chat in private since the *buwe* arrived. I want to hear what your friend Dorcas had to say when she saw you in *kurrich* yesterday."

"Dorcas wasn't in *kurrich* yesterday. She was spending the weekend with her *familye* in Serenity Ridge. I don't know if she's back yet." Susannah distractedly looked out the window and suddenly she was struck with an idea: she'd *walk* to the market to pick up more bacon and sausage for tomorrow's breakfast.

She thought she'd come up with the perfect way to get some exercise, but Lydia argued, "All the way on the other side of West River Road? That's too far and too dangerous. There's no shoulder on that road—an *Englisch* high school *bu* was recently hit riding his bike there. Your grandfather will insist you take the buggy."

Lydia was right; although most Amish men and women considered traveling by foot to be an integral part of their daily routine, Marshall had always been concerned about where and how far his granddaughter walked, especially in New Hope. Aware he wasn't going to budge on the issue, Susannah gave in. "Okay," she said with a sigh. "I'll take the buggy to the store."

"While we're talking about shopping, I noticed you didn't buy any beef. Weren't you planning on making sloppy joes for lunch?"

"*Jah.* But I'm using ground turkey, not beef." Susannah had memorized her favorite sloppy joe recipe, which also included a homemade sauce, carrots and green peppers.

"Oh, so that's what that turkey is for." Lydia wrinkled her nose. "I suppose that's okay, but it doesn't seem like you'll have nearly enough to feed five *hungerich menner.*"

"Five?" Susannah nearly shouted. "I didn't know Benuel and Peter were coming for lunch today!"

"They're coming for lunch *every* day. I thought I told you that you'd be cooking for the whole crew?"

What she'd thought Lydia said was that she'd be cooking for the out-of-town crew, referring to Conrad and Jacob, since Susannah hadn't known Benuel was coming from Serenity Ridge. "I guess I misunderstood. I figured Benuel and Peter would bring their own lunches."

"Neh. I can't let them eat a cold lunch while we're all in here enjoying a hot meal. I just wouldn't hear of it," Lydia declared. But her voice softened as she added, "We'll make do for this afternoon and you'll be going to the market later, anyway, so you can supplement what you bought on *Samschdaag.* There's no need to look so upset, dear."

Jah, there is, Susannah thought, close to tears at the notion of dining with Peter on a daily basis. But almost immediately, she consoled herself with the knowledge that there wouldn't be enough room at the table for all seven of them. So Susannah could claim she was too busy serving to sit down with everyone else. "I'd already planned to make a salad but I suppose I could supplement our lunch with more vegetables," she proposed.

"Jah—how about mashed potatoes?"

"I was thinking of roasted cauliflower and broccoli."

"Neh, potatoes are more filling. They're the perfect thing to have on the first day of harvest." Lydia looked out the window. "I see Peter and Benuel are loading the barrels into the buggy wagon—if you hurry, you can catch them before they leave and ask them to fill a basket for you now."

"That's okay. I'll go out and pick some myself after you've finished your *kaffi*."

"*Neh*, don't wait on my account—you've been itching to get outside. Besides, I told Marshall to *kumme* in for lunch at twelve thirty, so you've got a lot of peeling to do before then."

Susannah knew it was useless to protest once Lydia had made up her mind. *I'm going to have to see Peter every day at lunch, anyway. I might as well get used to it*, she silently conceded as she opened the door and stepped outside into the crisp autumn air.

Peter and Benuel finished heaving the last of the barrels onto the buggy wagon. It was Peter's turn to transport them to the potato house, where he'd unload them alone while Benuel would continue to help Conrad and Jacob pick in the fields. When Peter returned, he'd help pick, too. Once they had enough barrels to fill the buggy wagon again, they'd load it up together and then it would be Benuel's turn to go to the potato house. Because he was aware that an injured worker could significantly derail the harvesting schedule, Marshall insisted the two men alternate their transportation responsibilities like this throughout the day. He wanted each of them to have an opportunity to rest their arm and back muscles as they rode home from the storage building.

As he was checking to make sure the barrels were secure, Peter happened to notice something move in his peripheral vision. He glanced up to see Susannah approaching from the direction of the house.

"*Guder mariye*," she said when she reached them and they greeted her back. Her tone was polite but cool as she explained, "Lydia sent me to get potatoes for lunch."

Since Peter was standing in the buggy wagon and he had easy access to the barrels, he extended his hand to take the basket from her. But Benuel intercepted it and hopped up into the bed of the wagon, too. "How many do you need?" he asked.

"That depends on how many you think you'll eat. I'm making mashed potatoes for lunch."

"In that case, I'll fill it up."

Marshall must have invited Benuel to eat with the familye, Peter thought. While he himself hadn't expected to have lunch with them, it seemed strange that he'd be the only one who was excluded. No matter what Marshall thought of him, it just wasn't the Amish way to leave one person out. *It's almost as if I'm being shunned,* he thought. But then it occurred to him that perhaps Benuel had forgotten his cooler today.

Whistling as he chose the biggest potatoes, Benuel placed them in the basket and then jumped back down from the wagon right beside Susannah. "This should be enough for me. Did you bring another basket for the rest of the crew?" he joked.

She chuckled. "*Neh,* just the one. And a word to the wise—you'd better take as much as you want the first time the bowl is passed, because with Jacob and Conrad at the table, it won't *kumme* around a second time."

"I'll keep that in mind." Benuel grinned and presented her the basket. Was Peter mistaken or did he deliberately touch her fingers before he let go of its handle?

"Denki," Susannah replied and quickly pivoted back toward the house.

Watching her go, Benuel remarked, "She might just be the prettiest *maedel* I've ever seen."

Surprised to hear his coworker openly express a sentiment most Amish men would consider worldly, Peter replied, "She's not a *maedel*—she's a *weibsmensch*."

"*Jah*, you can say that again," Benuel said. "A very beautiful *weibsmensch*. Jacob and Conrad said she used to be on the plump side, but she sure isn't now. Do you know if she's got a suitor back in Maryland?"

Peter was so appalled by Benuel's brazen references to Susannah's appearance—to *any* woman's appearance and especially to her figure—all he could think to do was correct Benuel, as he replied, "Delaware. She lives in Delaware."

Benuel snickered. "Okay, does she have a suitor in Delaware, then?"

"How would I know?" Peter snapped. He climbed down from the wagon bed, strode around to the front of the buggy and pulled himself up onto the seat, ready to depart. But at the last second, he decided he couldn't let Benuel's remarks about Susannah go unaddressed. Over his shoulder, he cautioned, "You'd better not let Marshall hear you talking about Susannah like that. You might find yourself out of a job."

"*Denki* for the tip," Benuel called as Peter steered the horse toward the lane leading to the road. "I'll make sure he's not within earshot."

Peter hadn't really been suggesting Benuel should be careful Marshall didn't hear him talking about Susannah—he'd been suggesting Benuel shouldn't talk about Susannah at all. Especially not in such a boorish, superficial way.

Admittedly, he could understand why Benuel found

Susannah so attractive. Last summer, when Peter spotted her in church, he'd noticed her curly hair and fair, flawless skin, too. But it was her eyes had that made him go weak in the knees the first time they'd met. And it wasn't just because they were a striking, golden shade of brown; it was also because of the openness and warmth he'd seen in them.

Now she can't even bear to glance in my direction, he thought. Once again, he didn't blame her for that, but it bothered him that someone as bold as Benuel was vying for her attention. His comment about Susannah's weight was something he might have expected from an *Englischer*, not from a fellow Amish man. While it may have registered somewhere in the back of Peter's mind that Susannah seemed thinner than she had last Christmas, he hadn't given it a second thought until Benuel brought it to his attention again.

Maybe it was because he was too nervous in her presence to notice anything else, but the only thing that struck Peter as being different about Susannah's appearance was how rigid her posture was. It troubled him to know *he* was the reason she was standing as if her spine were a steel rod.

But at least I didn't say anything else dumm *to upset her just now*, he consoled himself. Of course, he hadn't said anything at all, but even that was an improvement from the last couple of times they'd interacted.

Once he reached the potato house, which was built into the side of a hill, half underground, half above, Peter emptied the barrels into a chute. Then he stacked the empty containers in the back of the buggy wagon and returned to the farm. His stomach had been growling for the last hour, so he was relieved when he saw the other four men going toward the house. *Must be time for our lunch break*, he surmised. It turned out just as well that Benuel had been invited to eat inside the house; Peter didn't want to have to listen to him make any more churlish remarks about Susannah while he was enjoying his own lunch.

After stabling the horse, he grabbed his cooler from his buggy and went to sit beneath a maple tree, leaning against its trunk. He closed his eyes to say grace and to pray for his mother's energy to return. But he opened them again when someone gave the sole of his boot a tap. It was Marshall.

Oh, wunderbaar. *He probably thinks I was sleeping on the job.* Peter jumped to his feet. "Sorry. I thought everyone was inside taking a lunch break."

"They are. And Lydia won't let us eat until you join us, so c'mon."

Peter understood: just as Susannah had made it clear it wasn't her idea to come and get potatoes from him and Benuel, Marshall was making it clear that it wasn't his idea to invite Peter to lunch. It was Lydia's. Susannah wasn't going to feel any more comfortable having Peter in the kitchen than he'd feel about being there, but he knew better than to insult Marshall's wife by turning down the offer of a good hot meal. He picked up his cooler and raced after the old man, who had already strode halfway back to the porch.

"I found him sleeping beneath a tree," Susannah's grandfather announced when he came through the door, with Peter lagging behind him, holding a cooler in his hands.

"I—I was saying grace. I didn't expect to be invited

in for lunch. I brought my own," he said apologetically, wiping his boots on the rug.

"There's no invitation needed. It's expected that we'll all eat lunch together every day, so you can leave that cooler at home from now on," Lydia said.

"*Denki*, that's very kind of—"

"Quit yakking and go wash your hands. We're *hungerich*," Marshall interrupted him.

Susannah noticed the color rise in Peter's cheeks. Groossdaadi *is too grumpy sometimes. I'm not* hallich *Peter is going to be eating with us every day, but at least he has the* gut *manners to express his appreciation...and to wipe his boots, which no one else took the time to do.* "The bathroom is on the right," she told him, pointing down the hall.

After he returned and they'd said grace, the men dug in to their food with gusto. For several minutes, no one spoke because their mouths were too full. Then, as their eating slowed, Marshall commented that he was pleased the crop seemed abundant so far and Lydia remarked how good the potatoes tasted.

"*Jah*, but next time, you should make more," Jacob told Susannah, scraping a spoon against the bottom of the serving dish to get every last trace of the white, creamy, mashed vegetable.

"Aren't you going to leave any for Susannah? She hasn't eaten yet," Benuel reminded the teenager. Then he caught her eye and offered, "If I scoot over, there should be room for you to squeeze in here."

Susannah was unnerved by his audacity; if she was going to sit at the table, she would have sat on the other side of Lydia, not next to Benuel. She'd found it awkward when he'd stood so close to her beside the buggy wagon and again when his hand had touched hers as she took the basket of potatoes from him. But she'd questioned whether he'd overstepped his boundaries accidentally or on purpose. Now that he'd suggested she should "squeeze in" next to him, she had no doubt he was behaving flirtatiously. And right in front of Lydia, too—what was he thinking? It was a good thing her grandfather had excused himself to the restroom.

"I don't want potatoes and I don't want to sit down next to you, either," she replied curtly. Then, seeing Lydia lower her eyebrows disapprovingly at her, she added, "*Denki*, but I'll eat later, after everyone has been served. Otherwise I'll be jumping up and down throughout the meal to bring things to the table."

"You mean like dessert?" Conrad hinted.

"I didn't make dessert but I thought you might like this yogurt, since no one ate any at breakfast," Susannah told him, placing the bowl on the table.

"There's a reason no one ate any of it for breakfast," Conrad muttered facetiously.

"It's not that bad when you add honey to it," his brother informed him, spooning a big swirl of honey into his bowl.

"I like yogurt. It's kind of like custard," Benuel said, but Susannah noticed he only took a small dollop.

"*Jah*, the consistency is the same. But the taste?" Lydia grimaced to demonstrate what she thought of it. Until Susannah started paying more attention to what she herself ate, she had never realized how finicky her stepgrandmother was about food.

"*What* taste? That stuff doesn't *have* any taste." Conrad's remark caused Lydia and Jacob to chuckle.

Susannah couldn't believe that they were making

such a fuss over yogurt; it wasn't as if she'd served them one of the appetizers she'd read about in the *Englisch* cookbooks, such as escargot or baby squid. She was just about to tell them she wouldn't buy plain yogurt again if eating it was such a hardship, when Peter spoke up for the first time since sitting down at the table.

"I remember one time when I was a young *bu* and I complained that I disliked what we were having for supper. My mother said, 'At this table, mouths may be used for eating, conversing or thanking the Lord for what He has provided us. Since you want to use your mouth to complain, you may go out into the barn and complain to the pig until we're done eating our dessert.'" Peter licked his spoon and chuckled. "I didn't make that mistake twice."

His point taken, everyone laughed good-naturedly. As he plopped a second heaping spoonful of yogurt onto his dish, Susannah begrudgingly admitted to herself, *Maybe having Peter around at lunchtime isn't quite so* baremlich, *after all. At least he can have a* gut *influence on the others' manners, which might make it easier for me to serve healthier food.*

But that didn't mean she wasn't glad when her grandfather returned to the room and told the men it was time for all of them to get back to work, including Peter, who hadn't even finished eating his yogurt yet.

Chapter Four

On Thursday afternoon, when Lydia mentioned she was tired because her cast had interfered with her sleep the evening before, Susannah encouraged her to take a nap in the recliner. As she positioned a pillow beneath her stepgrandmother's arm, trying to help her find a comfortable position, she felt a bit guilty because she knew she had an ulterior motive for convincing Lydia to rest: Susannah wanted to sneak in a walk before it started to rain.

All week, Lydia had found one excuse or the other to keep Susannah inside the house with her, whether it was that she needed Susannah to do some mending or to write a letter to Lydia's sister, or simply to keep her company while she was drinking tea—and usually eating a snack—in the afternoon. Susannah didn't mind helping her stepgrandmother with whatever she needed; after all, that was her purpose in coming to New Hope. And she understood why Lydia felt frustrated and restless. However, after four straight days of being with each other virtually all the time, except during her solo trip to the market, Susannah felt frustrated and restless, too.

Several times she'd invited Lydia to go for a walk with her, but her stepgrandmother usually came up with an excuse for why they should both stay inside instead. Once or twice, she'd convinced Lydia to sit on the porch swing while she cleaned the chicken coop or did a little yardwork nearby, but Susannah was itching to really stretch her legs.

I'll take the clothes off the line and then I'll walk down the lane to the mailbox and back again, but instead of stopping at the haus, *I'll continue toward the far, southern edge of* Groossdaadi's *property. I can repeat the loop twice if I hurry,* she schemed as she picked up the laundry basket and crept out onto the porch.

To her surprise, Susannah found Dorcas climbing the stairs. She set down the laundry basket so she could greet her friend with a hug. "It's so *gut* to finally see you!" she exclaimed as they embraced.

"It's *wunderbaar* to see you, too. But your shoulders feel so bony." Dorcas stepped back and eyed her. "You've lost quite a bit of weight. Have you been ill?"

"*Neh*, I'm healthier than ever. I wrote that I've changed my eating habits and I feel a lot stronger and more energetic lately, remember?"

"I remember you writing that you'd made changes to your *familye*'s diet because of your *daed*'s diabetes, but you never said anything about losing weight yourself." Dorcas frowned and smoothed her apron over her stomach, as if to push her round belly flatter, too.

"It didn't seem like it was worth mentioning," Susannah said dismissively. In fact, it would have felt boastful. "But I can't wait to hear what's new with you. *Kumme*, let's walk to the mailbox and you can tell me what has been happening in your life since you last wrote."

"Can't we sit on the swing instead?"

Susannah had already descended the porch steps. "Lydia is inside taking a nap. I don't want to disturb her."

"I don't know how we'd disturb her—the windows are closed and we're not going to shout," Dorcas grumbled, but she followed Susannah, anyway. As they walked down the long dirt driveway, Dorcas told her about her recent trip to Serenity Ridge to visit her aunt, uncle and cousins. "My *gschwischderkind* Hadassah is three years younger than I am and she told me she's getting married this *hochzich* season. And my *gschwischderkind* Sarah is only seventeen and she's already courting. At this rate, I'm going to be the spinster of the *familye*."

"There are worse things in life than being single."

"*Jah*, I know that. But, *Gott* willing, I still want to fall in love, get married and start a *familye* of my own. You do, too, don't you?"

Susannah shrugged. "Not especially. Not anymore."

"Really?" Dorcas glanced over at her, raising an eyebrow. "That's a big change from when you and Peter were courting. You wrote that you could hardly wait to become a wife and a *mamm*. Don't tell me you gave up your heart's desire to be married just because one *mann* didn't think you were a *gut* match for him."

Neh, what I really gave up was my hope that any mann *would love me unconditionally, for who I truly am*, Susannah thought, but she didn't express her feelings aloud. Even though she and Dorcas had become close confidantes, as well as pen pals, there were some heartaches Susannah couldn't share with anyone else. Instead, she said, "Speaking of Peter, did you know he's helping my *groossdaadi* and Lydia's great-nephews harvest the potato crop?"

Dorcas abruptly stopped walking. "He *is*?"

"*Jah*. There's another man on the crew, too. You might know him since he's from Serenity Ridge. His name is Benuel Heiser."

"*Jah*, I know him all right." Dorcas lowered her voice even though they were the only ones on the lane and explained that her cousins had told her Benuel had only ended his *rumspringa* last April, even though he was twenty-four. He'd spent several years living among the *Englisch* before finally returning to his family and being baptized into the church. Apparently, he'd made quite a bit of money by partnering with a couple of *Englischers* in buying houses, remodeling them and then selling them at a higher price in several of Maine's wealthier seaside vacation communities.

But after returning to New Hope for good, he'd made a commitment to work solely for Amish businesses as a way of completely cutting ties with his old *Englisch* lifestyle. Unfortunately, jobs within the small Serenity Ridge Amish community were difficult to come by, so Benuel took whatever work he could find. "I can understand why he'd help on your *groossdaadi*'s *bauerei*, but why would Peter join the crew when he has a business of his own to manage?"

"Peter knows a lot about harvesting potatoes. Before my *groossdaadi*'s *bruder*, Amos, died and left *Groossdaadi* the *bauerei*, Peter used to help with both planting and harvesting. He was a lot younger then, but I'm sure he still remembers. So I assume he agreed to help now as a favor because Lydia's *seh* couldn't *kumme* this season." Susannah tugged on Dorcas's sleeve to keep her moving; this was supposed to be a brisk walk, not a leisurely stroll.

"Maybe." Dorcas started forward again, but she still wasn't matching Susannah's pace. "Or maybe it's because he heard *you* were returning to New Hope. Maybe he wanted a second chance at courting you, so he thought this would be a *gut* way to be around you again."

"Ha! As if I'd ever accept him as a suitor again."

"You wouldn't? Not ever?"

"*Neh.* Never. But that's not why he's working on the *bauerei*. He didn't know I'd be here. He seemed as shocked to see me as I was to see him."

"You've already seen each other?"

"Not only have I seen him, but I've eaten lunch with him every day." Susannah told her that Lydia had insisted all of the crew members eat together. After the first day, she'd asked Marshall to add another leaf to the table so there would be room for Susannah to join them, too. As if that weren't awkward enough, Lydia had decided her granddaughter should sit in between Benuel, who was overly friendly, and Peter, who hardly said a word to her—nor did she speak to him unless it was absolutely necessary. Susannah thought the situation would have made her feel too flustered to eat anything at all, but instead she'd been nervously cramming food into her mouth, barely noticing how it tasted or how much she'd consumed.

"Was Peter surprised about your weight loss?"

"As I said, we've hardly spoken to each other. But

judging from the fact he didn't even recognize me when he saw me, *jah*, I'd say he was surprised."

Dorcas gleefully rubbed her hands together. "That must have been so satisfying!"

Neh, it was actually quite hurtful, Susannah thought. "I didn't lose weight for other people's approval. I changed my *familye*'s diet so we'd be healthier. And because I've *kumme* to realize how important it is to take care of the bodies *Gott* has given us."

"I know, I know. But considering how devastated you were when Peter broke up with you because you were overweight, I'd think it would feel *gut* to show him how thin you've become. Admit it—didn't you feel a tiny bit smug?"

"You mean prideful? *Neh*, I can honestly say I didn't." Susannah used her chin to gesture toward the buggy coming up the road. "Shh. That might be him returning from the potato *haus* now."

But as the buggy neared, she saw it was Benuel, not Peter, holding the reins. He slowed the horse to a halt just before he reached them and gazed down at Susannah. "Hi, Susannah. Who's your friend?"

Before Susannah could respond, Dorcas said, "You know who I am, Benuel. We've met several times in Serenity Ridge."

He pushed back his hat and squinted at her. "Ah, right. Sorry, Naomi."

"My name is *Dorcas*," Susannah's friend huffed.

Ignoring her disgusted reaction, Benuel addressed Susannah. "Do you need a ride somewhere?"

"*Neh*. We're enjoying our walk. Besides, my *groossdaadi* is paying you to transport potatoes, not passengers." Susannah intended to remind Benuel in a lighthearted way that he had work to do, but he seemed to think she was bantering with him.

"Maybe, but how can he blame me for wanting to take you for a ride when your eyes are so much prettier than a potato's?" Benuel replied with a wink.

Susannah's cheeks blazed from embarrassment. Speechless, she twirled and took off in the direction of the mailbox, with Dorcas in close pursuit. After hearing Benuel's wagon depart in the opposite direction, Susannah spluttered, "Can you believe how gutsy he is? He must have picked up that brash attitude from the *Englisch* during his extended *rumspringa*. They might think that kind of remark is complimentary, but I find it utterly offensive."

"You think *you're* offended?" Dorcas exclaimed. "I've been personally introduced to him at least three times in the past four months and he didn't have any clue what my name is. Plus, he flirted with you right in front of me. It's as if I'm invisible, which is *narrish*, considering I take up a lot more space than you do."

"Don't make jokes like that, Dorcas."

"Who's joking? It's the truth and you know it. Benuel acted as if I don't exist because he doesn't think I'm as attractive as you are."

"That's *lecherich*. Beauty is in the eye of the beholder."

"Exactly—and in *his* eyes, I'm too heavy to be beautiful."

Sadly, Susannah knew Dorcas was probably right about Benuel's perspective, so instead of denying it, she said, "If that's true, then I wish I was heavy again—it would be better than being the object of his flirtatious remarks. Or the object of *anyone's* remarks."

"You don't really expect me to believe that, do you?" Dorcas asked as Susannah retrieved the mail from the box. "I mean, I know Benuel comes on too strong, but I'm sure other people have complimented you on your weight loss and appearance. You have to admit, it must be encouraging to hear such positive comments."

"I won't admit any such thing because it's not true," Susannah countered defensively. "I wish people would stop talking about my weight altogether."

"Fine with me," Dorcas said, and Susannah recognized the edge to her voice. She'd heard it in other people's voices before, but she made no apology for her request. The women walked in silence until they almost reached the house again. It was beginning to drizzle, but Susannah figured if they hurried, they could make it to the tree line and back before the skies really opened up.

"Let's keep walking," she suggested. "I've been cooped up in the *haus* all week. Lydia never wants to go outside and she doesn't want me to go out, either."

"Shouldn't we take your laundry in first?"

"It'll be okay." Wheedling her friend, Susannah said, "When we get back we'll go inside for tea and you can have some of the oatmeal *kuche* I made, too."

"Oh, so you think you can bribe your chubby friend into exercising by offering her *kuche*?"

"*Neh.* That's not why I—"

Dorcas nudged Susannah's arm. "I'm only kidding. Of course, we can keep walking if it means that much to you. The extra exercise would be *gut* for me, too."

"*Denki.*" The tension between them dissolved, and Susannah admitted how challenging it was to spend nearly every minute of the day in Lydia's company.

"Then you ought to *kumme* to the work frolic my

schweschdere and I are organizing for Elizabeth Hilty on *Samschdaag*. She's been in the hospital with pneumonia but she's coming home on *Muundaag*. So some of the *weibsleit* from our district are cleaning her *haus* and stocking her freezer with meals that we'll prepare in her kitchen, since her husband will be away visiting her in the hospital all day."

"That sounds like *schpass*. I'd love to join you, as long as I can bring Lydia with me. She won't be able to do much, but she'll probably appreciate being around other *weibsleit* as much as I will."

As they discussed the details of the work frolic, it began drizzling harder. Even though they hadn't reached the tree line yet, Susannah conceded that they should return to the house. They'd barely gone twenty yards when the clouds burst, pelting them with a torrent of raindrops.

"The clothes!" Remembering the laundry on the line, Susannah was delighted for the excuse to break into a sprint. "We'd better make a dash for it."

"They're going to be drenched no matter how quickly we get there," Dorcas objected. "And so are we. Wet is wet."

"Dawdle if you want, but I'm going to run. I'll meet you back there." Susannah charged forward, head down. She loved running like this, her heart beating so hard she could hear it in her ears, her breathing heavy, her feet slapping the damp ground. Because she'd previously been overweight for so long, she hadn't run this fast since she was a young girl, and as she barreled forward, she felt as vibrant and powerful as a wild horse.

"Whoa!" someone said just as that thought entered her mind.

Susannah glanced up to see Peter standing frozen, hands out, palms up, directly in her path. Attempting to stop, she skidded across the wet dirt, almost as if on ice skates, before thudding backward onto her rump. Although she broke her fall with the palms of her hands, she landed so hard she bounced, but even that didn't hurt her physically as much as it wounded her pride.

"Are you all right?" he asked, towering above her.

"Jah," she replied, too abashed to look up at him. She reached behind her head to refasten her prayer *kapp*, trying to gather her composure. While she was pinning it into place, Peter opened the black umbrella he'd had tucked beneath his arm and held it above her, shielding her from the rain. He offered her his free hand but she rose to her feet without any help from him. A moment later, Dorcas joined them.

"Are you okay, Susannah?" She was either panting or laughing…or a little bit of both.

"Jah." Susannah couldn't say the same for the skirt of her dress, which was dirty, as well as wet.

Dorcas turned her attention to Peter. "Hello." She greeted him cordially, as if they were at a singing instead of standing in the pouring rain. "I'm surprised to see you here on the farm. I thought your business would keep you too busy to help Marshall with the harvest."

Susannah didn't appreciate Dorcas's line of questioning and she started walking—limping, actually—toward the house. She'd rather get soaked to the bone than walk beneath the umbrella with Peter. He and Dorcas followed closely enough that she was still within earshot of their conversation.

"I—I agreed last winter I'd help him. Hannes can

manage the shop without me since this is a slow time of year for picnic-table orders."

"Oh. I see. Well, that's nice of you." Dorcas's voice sounded sweeter than usual. Almost lilting. "Why did you *kumme* to this part of the farm? I didn't see anyone else out this way."

Susannah had wondered the same thing, but she'd been too humiliated from taking a spill to ask.

"Lydia saw me bringing some barrels into the barn and she called me over to take the umbrella to you two. She'd noticed it was drizzling and she was concerned you'd get wet."

"Ha!" Susannah sputtered. Lydia's matchmaking attempts were *so* obvious. Over her shoulder she remarked, "She should have been more concerned I'd get muddy. Why didn't you move out of my way when you saw me coming?"

"There wasn't enough time. I heard footsteps, glanced up and there you were, heading toward me like a freight train."

For as much weight as she'd lost, Susannah still bristled at being compared to a freight train. Dorcas, however, cracked up. "You really were running full steam ahead, Susannah. I didn't have time to call out a warning to either of you." She giggled again, then asked Peter, "Are you *menner* done picking potatoes for the afternoon?"

"*Jah.* The rain looks like it's going to keep up for a while and we don't want the potatoes to sprout or rot. So we'll wait until the sky is clear tomorrow and the ground has had a chance to dry."

"In that case, do you mind giving me a ride home?

I don't have an umbrella and unlike my friend Susannah here, I get a little chilly from walking in the rain."

"We're going to have tea—that should warm you up," Susannah reminded her. "And I can give you a ride home afterward."

"Won't you need to start supper, since your *groossdaadi* is coming in early?"

It almost seemed as if Dorcas actually preferred to go with Peter. "I'm sure *Groossdaadi* won't mind if I serve supper at our usual time."

"No need for that," Peter said. "Your *haus* is on my way, Dorcas. I'm *hallich* to give you a ride. I've got to help stable the *geil* and put away the equipment so it will be a few minutes before we can leave."

"That's fine. I'll be ready whenever you are." There it was again, that dulcet tone. Why was Dorcas being so sweet to Peter?

She must be trying to compensate for my brusqueness, Susannah thought as he walked away and the two women pulled the wet clothes from the line. Instead of feeling sorry for being inhospitable toward Peter, she resented Dorcas's affability. *It's easy enough for her to act so pleasant to him. She's not the one whose heart he broke. And she's not the one he caused to fall on her backside, either!*

When Susannah and Dorcas entered the house, Lydia was right there at the door with a dry towel for each of them. Apparently, she'd watched the entire scene unfold from the window. "Why didn't you walk beneath the umbrella with Peter and Dorcas?" she asked incredulously. "And why were you running in the first place? You're fortunate you didn't end up falling and breaking *your* wrist, too. Then what would we have done?"

I would have been able to go back to Delaware, Susannah thought. A broken wrist seemed like a small price to pay for the freedom of being able to take a nice long walk outdoors whenever she wanted—especially if it meant she could take that nice long walk in a state that was six hundred miles away from Peter.

"Where have you been?" Marshall asked when Peter reached the barn. Benuel was nowhere in sight and Conrad and Jacob were wiping mud and grease from the mechanical potato digger.

"Lydia asked me to bring Susannah and her friend an umbrella." Peter hoped that by mentioning it was Lydia's idea, he'd spare himself a lecture from Marshall, but he was wrong.

"You're not here to run errands or socialize with the *weibsleit*—you're here to help with the harvest," Marshall retorted. "The crew took care of stabling the *geil* and bringing in the equipment. You can gather the rest of the empty barrels, wipe them dry and turn them upside down. C'mon, *buwe*, let's go inside for a hot drink and something to eat."

Peter waited until they'd left to walk back out into the rain himself. The water dripped off the rim of his hat and ran down his back, but he didn't mind. *It's not as if I'm going to melt, the way Lydia seems to worry Susannah will*, he thought.

He didn't understand Lydia and Marshall's protectiveness toward their granddaughter. They coddled her as if she was an infirm child instead of a healthy adult woman. Except for when she was hanging out or taking in the laundry, Peter had rarely caught sight of her outdoors this week. She didn't even pick the potatoes she served at lunchtime—Benuel did it for her.

Up until this afternoon, Peter had entertained the possibility that she'd been ill; maybe that was why she'd lost weight. But seeing her bolting toward him faster than lighting a few minutes ago had eliminated that question from his mind. There was clearly nothing wrong with her health.

Is it that she's spoiled? Or...lazy? Although pride was considered one of the worst—if not *the* worst—character traits an Amish person could have, laziness was a close second. Peter felt judgmental for even contemplating whether Susannah lacked a strong work ethic. After all, he suspected that's how some people viewed his mother and nothing could have been further from the truth. Besides, the summer they were courting, Peter had seen Susannah at plenty of work frolics and she'd always been very industrious.

Whatever Susannah does or doesn't do while she's at her groossdaadi*'s haus is really none of my business*, he reminded himself as he stacked the half barrels on top of each other so he could make fewer return trips to the barn. But what *was* his business was how Susannah treated *him*.

Even though Peter knew he was at fault for having wronged her—for having broken up with her without giving her any real reason—it still bothered him that she clearly couldn't stand to be in his company. At lunchtime, she always inched her chair as far from him as she possibly could without bumping into Benuel on her other side. The most she'd ever spoken to him while they were eating was to ask him to pass the pepper.

And just now she'd demonstrated further evidence of

her revulsion toward him by refusing to accept his offer
to help her toward her feet. *She'd rather sit in the mud
than touch my hand*, he thought. So much had changed
since the previous Christmas, when they'd both walked
three miles in twenty-degree weather just so they could
spend one hour alone with each other at Little Loon
Pond. As frigid as the weather had been, they'd removed
their gloves to hold hands because it seemed more romantic that way…

Peter shivered and glanced up at the darkening sky.
*If this rain keeps up, we won't be able to pick potatoes
tomorrow, either*, he thought. While he'd appreciate
giving his back and shoulder muscles a break from the
arduous labor, Peter wished they could finish harvesting as soon as possible.

Dear Gott, *please help me have a better attitude
about keeping my end of the agreement I made with
Marshall*, he silently prayed. *I know that without his financial help, Hannes might have gone to jail. So please
help me to be more grateful for this opportunity and to
complete it in a way that honors You. And please show
me what to do or say to help Susannah feel more comfortable about my presence on the farm.*

As it was, Peter hoped that by offering to take Dorcas
home, he'd be sparing Susannah the inconvenience of
hitching the horse and taking her friend home herself.
In turn, Marshall's supper wouldn't be delayed. But
twenty minutes later, when he went up to the house to
tell Dorcas he was ready to leave, Peter regretted his
offer of transportation.

"She'll be out in a minute," Marshall told him, stepping onto the porch. Once he'd closed the door behind
him, he added in a low voice, "As long as you keep away

from Susannah, it's none of my business who you court. But this is the last time I'll remind you that while you're on my *bauerei*, you're here to work, not to socialize."

Peter narrowed his eyes. What was Marshall talking about? Then it dawned on him: he thought Peter was interested in Dorcas and that's why he was giving her a ride home. The notion was preposterous—not because Dorcas wasn't a perfectly kind and winsome woman. But because even if he didn't think of her in a sisterly sort of way, Peter had absolutely no inclination to strike up a courtship with her or anyone else, especially not under Marshall's watchful eye. Swallowing his indignation, Peter nodded his agreement, just as Dorcas came out of the house.

Whatever she chattered about on the way home went in one of Peter's ears and out the other; all he could think about was how wrong Marshall was about him. He'd been wrong about why Peter had needed money last winter and he was wrong about why Peter offered to give Dorcas a ride home this afternoon. And even though he'd just prayed that the Lord would give him a better attitude, Peter mentally wrestled with feelings of resentment all the way home.

By the time he arrived at his own house, he had half a mind to tell Hannes that *he* was going to have to finish harvesting the potato crop. If he didn't like it, that was just plain tough. As for Marshall's reaction, Peter supposed the old farmer would be pleased not to have to worry that Peter was going to waste valuable work time pursuing Susannah's friends. But he ultimately overcame the temptation to quit, knowing that it wouldn't have been the honorable thing to do, even if it seemed justifiable at the moment.

"Hi, Eva. Where are Hannes and *Mamm*?" he asked when he entered the kitchen.

"Hannes is doing the second milking. *Mamm*'s in bed."

"Already?"

"She's in bed *still*. Hannes said she stayed there all day. She was resting when I came home. I tried to get her to *kumme* into the kitchen and visit with me while I made supper but she didn't want to get up."

Peter went down the hall and knocked on his mother's bedroom door. When she didn't answer, he knocked again and then entered. "*Mamm?* Are you okay?"

She stirred but didn't sit up. "*Jah.* Just tired."

Although it was going to be dark soon, Peter raised the shades on both of her windows. "I know you are, *Mamm*, but it's important that you get out of bed each day unless you're actually physically ill."

"Mmm. I will. In a minute." But she pulled the covers over her shoulder and rolled over.

What would Daed *do if he were here?* Peter asked himself, rubbing his forehead. He supposed his father would have convinced Dorothy to go to the doctor. But Peter had no idea what his dad would have said to persuade her, and even though Peter was an adult, he believed it was still important to obey God's command to honor his parents. And right now that meant respecting his mother's wish to be left alone, so he turned and went to wash up before supper.

While the three siblings were eating their meal—fried fish Eva had purchased from the frozen-food section at the market—she asked, "What did Susannah serve today?"

Ever since Peter had told his sister that Susannah

made lunch for the crew, Eva had become preoccupied with what she'd served them. Apparently, the summer he and Susannah were courting, she'd made blueberry crumb bars that had really left an impression on Peter's sister. "She called it cabbage-crust pizza."

"The crust was made out of cabbage?" Eva wrinkled her forehead. "Was it *gut*?"

"*Jah.* It was *appenditlich.*" Everything Susannah had made was delicious. To be honest, her meals were the highlight of Peter's day on the farm. Which was saying a lot, considering how nerve-racking it was to sit at the table with her on one side and Marshall on the other. But once he began eating, Peter would forget about everything except the taste of whatever meal she had prepared.

Apparently, the same was true for the other men, because even though Jacob and Conrad had complained about eating yogurt on Monday, they hadn't voiced any dissatisfaction since then and neither had Lydia. Benuel was especially complimentary about Susannah's cooking, but in general everyone would devour the food until the serving dishes were empty. They rarely had enough time to lean back in their chairs and pat their stomachs before Marshall would rush them out the door and into the fields.

"There's going to be a work frolic at the Hiltys' home on *Samschdaag* to make food and clean house for Elizabeth. I don't mind walking there and back, so do you care if I go?" Eva asked her brothers.

"*Mamm* shouldn't be left home alone," Peter objected.

"But can't Hannes look in on her like he usually does

when I'm in *schul*? She'll probably stay in bed most of the day, anyway."

Hannes chimed in, "That's fine with me. The shop's only open until two and I can take frequent breaks since we don't have any new orders to fill."

"None at all?" Peter had expected business to slow down at this time of year, but he didn't expect it to stop altogether. While they'd recovered from the financial setback after Hannes totaled the car, Peter hoped to pad their emergency-savings fund. Especially since they might need to dip into it if it turned out his mother had a severe health issue that required ongoing treatment.

"*Neh*. Not right now. But don't worry. I'm using our current supplies to get a jump on our next big order. I figure it's a way to save time without spending money."

While Peter was relieved that his brother was finally learning to take initiative, he still had qualms about Eva going off to a frolic and leaving their mother alone. Dorothy spent so much of the week by herself already and the weekends were a good opportunity for Eva to put in a little more effort to coax her out of bed.

"Please, Peter?" she pleaded, clasping her hands beneath her chin, her eyes filled with hope.

"Aw, you should let her go," Hannes commented to his brother. "You remember what it's like to be young and to want to socialize with your friends."

"*Jah*, you're right," Peter agreed, even though at the moment he felt so encumbered with concerns that he could hardly recall ever being young, and socializing was the last thing on his mind…no matter what Marshall Sommer believed about him.

Chapter Five

Susannah's grandfather had said he expected the rain to last until early Friday morning, but it kept up throughout the day, which meant the men couldn't harvest. In Delaware, Susannah lived with her father, brother, sister-in-law, and five nieces and nephews, so she was used to a bustling household. However, she hadn't realized quite how small her grandfather's house was until she had spent an entire day indoors with four other people. Not only was Lydia right there at her elbow every time Susannah turned around, but Susannah also felt as if she was constantly asking Jacob or Conrad to pull their feet in so she wouldn't trip as she passed by their chairs in the kitchen or living room.

Furthermore, even though they'd gotten far less physical activity than they would have picking potatoes, the teenagers were hungrier than they'd been all week. Susannah would just finish putting away the dishes from one meal when they'd ask if there was anything they could snack on until she made the next meal. Unfortunately, a couple of times she caught herself nibbling on the treats she'd prepared for them simply because she was antsy about being in such close quarters with everyone all day.

To add to her sense of the walls closing in, Lydia had said she didn't want to go to the frolic on Saturday. That meant Susannah had to stay home with her, as Lydia couldn't be—or wouldn't allow herself to be—left alone in the house for that amount of time.

So when Susannah woke on Saturday morning to the sound of drops pattering against the windowpanes, she was delighted. *This means I can go to the frolic after all, since* Groossdaadi*, Jacob and Conrad will be home with Lydia*, she thought.

She quickly got up and got dressed, but she noticed her skirt felt a little too snug around her waist. Like many Amish women, Susannah used straight pins instead of buttons to fasten her garments, so adjusting the closure for a more comfortable fit was easily done. However, it distressed Susannah that she needed to let out the skirt.

She went into the kitchen to begin making bread before anyone else woke up. As she was kneading the dough, she reflected on the meals she'd been preparing the last week. She had done her best to balance Lydia and Marshall's food preferences with healthier ingredients, and she'd been pleased that after Monday, they'd seemed content with what she'd served them. The trick, she'd learned, was to discreetly slip in or disguise the more nutritious substitutions—no small feat, considering Lydia shadowed her constantly.

However, she recognized from how bloated she'd become that she'd been eating too much. The lack of exercise didn't help matters, either. *Oh, well, at least I'll be walking to the Hiltys' haus today and I can just munch on vegetables for lunch, the way I'd do if I were home*, she planned.

She had zipped through her morning chores, including fixing breakfast, washing the dishes and sweeping the floors by nine thirty. She'd also prepared a cauliflower casserole that one of the boys could slide into the oven to bake for lunch, as Lydia wouldn't be able to manage the heavy pan on her own.

"I expect to leave the Hiltys' *haus* by three o'clock at the latest," she said as she put on her coat and grabbed an umbrella from the hook on the wall.

Her grandfather chuckled. "Slow down, Susannah. I haven't even hitched the *gaul* yet."

"No need to do that, *Groossdaadi*. I'm going to walk."

"In this weather?" Lydia asked, butting in. "We don't want *you* ending up with pneumonia, like Elizabeth did. Isn't that right, Marshall?"

"*Jah.* I'll go bring the buggy around."

Susannah was so exasperated she felt like screaming and stamping her foot, but then she would have been behaving as childishly as her grandparents were treating her. So she waited until she got into the buggy a few minutes later to discuss the subject in a calm, direct manner.

"You know, *Groossdaadi*, when I'm at home in Dover, I don't think twice about walking a few miles to the market or to my friend's *haus* if the buggy isn't available. I enjoy the fresh air and exercise. You really didn't need to trouble yourself to take me to the frolic."

"It's no trouble—it's my responsibility to take *gut* care of my *familye*. Our community is smaller and more spread out than yours is in Delaware and you aren't used to these roads."

Aha, I get it—Groossdaadi *isn't giving me a ride because he's treating me like a* kind *or because he's trying to stop me from doing what I want to do*, Susannah realized. *He's giving me a ride because he sees it as his responsibility as the head of his household.* Even though his perspective seemed old-fashioned to her, she appreciated his intentions. "*Denki* for looking out for me, *Groossdaadi*. I always feel very well-cared for when I *kumme* here."

Marshall cleared his throat. "Of course, there are more important ways of being a *gut* provider than giving a *weibsmensch* a ride in a buggy on a rainy day. Earning a decent living is one of them."

Now Susannah was perplexed. What was Marshall implying? He knew Susannah's father, a corn and soybean farmer, had frequently struggled to make ends meet. But while Susannah's family may have been among the poorer families in their district, she'd always believed they were one of the happiest.

Her grandfather looked straight ahead and adjusted his hat, as if he was embarrassed. "When it comes time for you to decide whether a young *mann* might make a suitable husband, I hope you'll consider his sense of financial responsibility, as well as his other qualities. For example, I happen to know that Benuel Heiser saved a good deal of the money he made while working with the *Englisch*. He may have made errors in judgment during his *rumspringa*, but he deserves credit for planning ahead about how to provide for a *familye* once he returned to the Amish."

Susannah couldn't help herself; she laughed out loud.

"I don't know what Lydia has told you, but trust me, *Groossdaadi*, I'm not assessing any *mann*, rich or poor, to determine if he'd make a *gut* husband." She glanced over at him and noticed his cheeks were crimson. His wife must have put him up to having this embarrassing conversation with his granddaughter, the poor man.

By way of changing the subject, Susannah began humming one of the hymns they'd sung at church the previous Sunday. After a few bars, they both began singing, loudly and slightly off-key, just like when they'd travel by buggy together when she was a young girl. And by the time she arrived at the Hiltys' house, Susannah had forgotten about her tight skirt or how frustrated she'd felt about Lydia thwarting her plans to walk to the frolic.

"Hi, Susannah," Dorcas said, greeting her at the door. "*Kumme* into the kitchen. We're having a snack before we get started."

Susannah had met most of the other women and teenage girls at church. And as the rest of them introduced themselves, she was glad Lydia had decided to stay home after all. This was a younger group of mostly unmarried women and she probably would have gotten restless and wanted to leave earlier than three o'clock.

"Do you want a cinnamon roll?" a woman named Faith asked, extending a pan. "I just finished icing them."

"She doesn't eat sweets," Honor answered before Susannah could speak up for herself.

It was true that last Sunday Susannah *had* told Honor that she didn't usually eat sweets anymore, which was stretching the truth a little, since she did have dessert on occasion. The reason she'd told her that was because

Honor had offered her a slice of pound cake that she'd brought to church…and Honor was a notoriously inept baker and cook. If Susannah was going to indulge, she wanted to thoroughly enjoy the treat. The cinnamon rolls that Faith had made smelled as tantalizing as they looked, so despite her expanding waistline, Susannah actually *did* want one.

"Oh, sorry." Faith turned and set the pan on the counter. "Is that how you got so skinny?"

"Susannah doesn't like it if you talk about her appearance," Dorcas interjected. She nonchalantly licked the top of her cinnamon roll as if it was an ice-cream cone. "She doesn't want people to think she's vain."

Susannah's mouth dropped open in surprise at her friend's remark. It almost seemed as if Dorcas was implying that Susannah *was* vain, but she didn't want people to *think* she was. *She still doesn't believe I'm uneasy receiving all of this uninvited attention.* Susannah thoughts were interrupted by a loud cracking noise in the hallway.

It was followed by the sound of a woman wailing. "Oh, *neh*! Look what I did!"

All of the women rushed into the hallway to find Hannah Miller scrutinizing a broken step on the staircase. Apparently, she'd brought her heel down on the edge of the board and had fractured the wood.

"David's a roof installer," Dorcas said, comforting her. "He'll be able to patch this up in no time."

"*Jah*, but he's been through such a hardship with his wife being hospitalized. The last thing he needs is to *kumme* home and have to mend something I broke. We're supposed to be making things easier for him, not more difficult."

"Listen." Susannah put a finger to her lips. "I just heard a buggy. I'll run out and see if one of the *menner* is dropping his *schweschder* or *dochder* off. Maybe it's someone who can fix the step."

She shot out the door and tore right past whatever young woman had been dropped off without registering who it was. Waving her arms as she pursued the buggy down the road, she hollered, *"Absatz!"* But the person at the reins didn't hear her and the horse increased its speed. Susannah increased hers, too, as well as her volume. *"Absatz!"* she shouted, chasing the buggy. She quickly realized whoever was in it couldn't hear her over the noise of the wheels and hooves on the pavement.

It wasn't until the buggy came to a halt at the intersection with the main thoroughfare that Susannah could make herself heard. Using the last of her lung power, she yelled, "Help!"

A man immediately hopped down from the carriage and raced toward her so swiftly that his hat flew off. It was Peter, of all people. "What's wrong? Is someone hurt? Are you all right?" he asked when he reached her, where she'd lost momentum some twenty yards behind his buggy.

She'd been galloping at such a fast clip and for such a long stretch she could hardly breathe. She bent over, pressing her palms against her thighs, and gasped in as much air as she could while holding one finger in the air to indicate she needed a minute.

"Take your time. It's okay. Take your time," Peter repeated, patiently waiting for her to catch her breath before she explained.

When Susannah peered over at him, she saw the

look of concern in his steel-blue eyes matched the tenderness of his tone. She remembered that expression; most memorably, she'd seen it on his face last summer, when he'd confided he was worried his brother was becoming influenced by his *Englisch* friends during his *rumspringa*. The depth of Peter's concern about the well-being of others—especially his family members—was one of the things she'd found particularly attractive about him.

However, that kind of worry was unwarranted in this instance. Susannah felt sheepish as she told him, "Someone accidentally broke a board on the staircase. No one's hurt but we were hoping you could fix it before David comes home."

It seemed to take a moment for the meaning of her words to sink in, and when it did, Peter shook his head and asked, "You ran all this way to ask me *that*?"

It was kind of a melodramatic impulse, now that she thought about it. Susannah could have just asked her grandfather to repair the broken stair when he returned to pick her up at three o'clock. But she wasn't thinking as she was sprinting after the buggy. It was as if her legs were rebelling after a week of idleness—as if she was somehow breaking free from Lydia's restrictive behavior—but when she'd been running, all that had mattered was catching up to the horse. "I—I'm sorry if I alarmed you," she feebly apologized.

"It's fine. I'll look at the step to see what I can do. It'll take a couple minutes to reverse my direction." He turned and walked back down the narrow road. When he neared his hat, he lifted it from the ground, clapped it against his palm and got into the carriage. Even though Susannah knew it was utterly irrational, since she hadn't exactly been courteous to him, she felt the tiniest bit slighted that he didn't offer to give her a ride back to the house.

"Did you catch my *bruder* in time?" Eva asked when Susannah opened the door and stepped onto the small braided rug. Honor was standing behind her in the hallway and the other women's voices could be heard coming from the kitchen.

"*Jah*, he's turning the buggy around."

"I'll get a towel. You're dripping and dirty and we've already scrubbed the gathering-room floor," Honor said. "Don't go anywhere."

Eva left, too, so Susannah removed her boots, and as she was waiting for Honor to return, Peter came in, toolbox in hand. Susannah moved to one side of the rug so he could take off his boots. He'd barely untied his laces when Dorcas came out of the kitchen, smiling. "*Denki* for coming back, Peter. *Kumme*, I'll show you the damage."

Peter followed her down the hall, out of sight, but Susannah could still hear their voices. "This won't be any problem," Peter said. "I have some boards this size left over from when I redid our staircase. I'll go get one and *kumme* back a few minutes before I pick Eva up at two o'clock so I don't have to make an extra trip."

"You should *kumme* at noon instead. That's when we're taking a break for lunch and we've got lots of *gut* food here," Dorcas offered, to Susannah's dismay. Having made a fool of herself chasing Peter down for help as if the house had been on fire, she wanted a little more time to pass before she had to sit down at a table with him again. But he accepted her invitation and then

Dorcas asked, "Would you like a cinnamon roll to take with you for now?"

Peter said something in a hushed tone that Susannah couldn't hear. However, Dorcas's melodic laughter rang out loud and clear. "Don't worry," she said. "It will be our little secret."

What will be their little secret? Susannah wondered as she heard footsteps coming down the staircase. Honor asked Peter if he'd take a look at the loose doorknob on the linen closet, too. A few seconds later, she came down the hall and handed Susannah a towel.

"You look like something the cat dragged in," she teased.

Susannah blotted her face, and the sleeves and hem of her dress, with the towel, then went into the bathroom. A glimpse in the mirror revealed her curly hair was fluffing up higher than ever, her prayer *kapp* was crooked and she had dirt smeared across both of her cheeks, which were blotchy from the exertion of running. *I look like something the cat* wouldn't *drag in*, she thought.

Despite claiming her appearance wasn't as important to her as it seemed to be to others, Susannah was disgusted with her reflection. She looked terrible and she *felt* terrible. Although she couldn't really put a finger on why, she suspected her low mood had something to do with the fact that her closest friend in New Hope had been laughing and sharing secrets with her former suitor. *Dorcas knows how deeply he hurt me*, Susannah thought. *Doesn't she have any sense of loyalty?* It wasn't that she expected Dorcas to ignore Peter, but Dorcas was being friendlier to him than she was being toward Susannah.

Then she wondered whether it was possible Peter and Dorcas liked each other. That didn't make any sense, though, because Dorcas was even heavier than Susannah had been at her heaviest. *Peter wouldn't have any romantic interest in a* weibsmensch *who weighs as much as Dorcas does and Dorcas wouldn't have any romantic interest in a* mann *who would reject a* weibsmensch *because of her weight*, she reassured herself. Not that she cared about who Peter courted, but Susannah didn't want Dorcas winding up feeling as crushed as she had felt.

When she emerged from the bathroom, she went into the kitchen. No one was in there; she could hear muffled voices coming from the rooms overhead. Noticing there was still half a pan of cinnamon rolls, she quickly pulled one of them from the loaf and took a huge bite. Icing dribbled down her chin. She dabbed it off and then licked her fingertip before taking another big bite of the roll. Three more bites and it was gone, but she'd eaten it so quickly she hardly tasted it, so she took another to enjoy at her leisure.

She'd only nibbled a third of the way through the cinnamon swirls to the sticky sweet center when she heard footsteps approaching. Panicked that she'd be caught eating the kind of food everyone thought she avoided, she shoved the rest of the bun into her mouth. Her cheeks felt as round as a chipmunk's, but her mouth was too full for her to move her jaw enough to chew the thick, soft dough.

As someone entered the kitchen, she twirled around toward the sink and picked up a clean glass, pretending she was washing it so she wouldn't have to face whoever had just come in.

Peter walked over and set his mug on the counter next to the sink. "Sorry," he said. "I know how frustrated my *schweschder* gets when she's almost done with dishes and someone brings her one more."

"Mmm." That was as close as she could come to pronouncing an actual word. Out of the corner of her eye, she saw him shift from foot to foot, but he didn't leave.

"I, um, I'm also sorry I caused you to fall the other day. I would have felt *baremlich* if you'd gotten hurt. I—I hope you'll forgive me since, you know, we'll be around each other on the *bauerei* for a few more weeks. I know things have been kind of awkward between us, but if there's anything that I can do to make you feel more comfortable about my presence there, I'll do it. Because I'd like it if we could be…more neighborly to one another."

Susannah couldn't answer him because her mouth was still too full, but how would she have responded, anyway? It would have been immature and unkind to tell him, *The only thing that would make me feel more comfortable about* your *presence on the* bauerei *would be my* absence *from it.*

There were too many people nearby, so she couldn't very well have added, *And you* did *hurt me, but not because you caused me to fall in the mud.* Besides, he knew how she'd felt when he'd broken up with her and he had already apologized that his decision had hurt her feelings.

Deep down, Susannah knew it was time to forgive him, to *really* forgive him. To ask the Lord to take the lingering hurt and anger she felt toward Peter and to help her to treat him in a way that reflected God's love instead of her unforgiving spirit. She still didn't think it was right for him to break up with her the way he had. But it was just as wrong for her to continue bearing a grudge against him…and for essentially expecting Dorcas to bear one, too. Especially since Peter had indicated he was willing to do whatever it took to make Susannah feel more comfortable around him for the duration of the harvest season.

She tried to say, *I'd like that, too.* Except her mouth was so full it came out more like "Erd wrikat ru."

In her peripheral vision, she could see Peter cocking his head and scrutinizing her. She managed to swallow a bit of the roll and then she covered her mouth with her hand and said, "I'd like that, too. I mean, I think we can be more neighborly to each other from now on."

"Gut." Peter nodded vigorously. He waited a moment, as if he expected her to say something else, but when she didn't, he told her he'd see her later and then he left the room.

As soon as she heard the front door close, Susannah went over to the trash bin and spat out the rest of the roll. She'd completely lost her desire for it, now that the Lord had replaced her bitter resentment with the sweet taste of forgiveness.

Denki, Gott, Peter silently prayed. He was so grateful that Susannah hadn't rebuffed him that he could have jumped up and clicked his heels together as he made his way back to the buggy. He'd asked the Lord to show him what to say or do to help her feel more comfortable around him. But until he saw Susannah standing alone by the sink, it hadn't occurred to Peter to ask *her* that same question.

It was such a relief to have directly addressed the

awkwardness between them. Granted, he didn't expect they'd suddenly engage in long, meaningful conversations or anything like that, but at least now Susannah might not recoil at the sight of him. And he wouldn't feel quite so tense around her, either, always afraid he'd say or do something to upset her even more.

He journeyed toward the other side of town and when he reached his family's property, he headed toward the house instead of the workshop. He had left a note telling his mother where everyone had gone, but he wanted to stop in to try to urge her to get up and have something to eat. But, to his astonishment, she was sitting in the living room, reading her Bible and drinking tea.

When he explained why he had to return to the Hiltys' home, she said, "Oh, *gut.* This gives me the opportunity to write a note for you to take for Elizabeth. I might not have the energy to help at the frolic, but I can still let her know I'm praying for her recovery."

Recognizing his window of opportunity—and feeling encouraged by how well Susannah had responded when he'd broached a difficult subject—Peter replied, "You know, *Mamm,* a different *dokder* might be able to help you regain your energy again so that you *can* go to frolics. And, more importantly, so you can start to feel better."

"Shush, *suh.* You're ruining my concentration," she said, waving her free hand at him as she inscribed a note card with the other. But Peter was heartened that she hadn't definitively refused to see a different doctor.

Maybe with a few well-timed suggestions, she'll agree to make an appointment, he thought an hour later as he made the return trip to the Hiltys' home with the board and tools he needed. Even before entering the house, he heard peals of laughter and he smiled to himself, imagining the fun Eva must have been having with her friends. But when he went inside, he was surprised to find Benuel was the one making the young women giggle.

"Hi," Peter greeted him. "I didn't expect to see you at this frolic."

"I came to pick up Emily."

Emily Heiser, a year older than Eva, was Benuel's cousin. "*Jah*, I recently started a job babysitting for an *Englisch familye*," she said. "I don't have to be there until two o'clock, but I think Benuel showed up early because I told him about all of the *gut* food we were making."

"What can I say? It's true," Benuel admitted with a shrug.

"We're freezing or storing most of what we made for Elizabeth and David, but we've set aside plenty for all of us, too. It'll be ready in a few minutes, if you *menner* want to fix the stair in the meantime," Hannah suggested.

So Benuel followed Peter to the staircase, even though it was really a one-man job. "Can you smell that? It's potato stuffing and beef and noodles." He inhaled deeply. "I saw whoopie pies in there, too. One of the things I really missed when I lived with the *Englisch* was our food. Amish *meed* cook a lot better than the *Englischers* do. Well, except maybe for Susannah."

"What?" Peter asked as he pried the nails from the cracked board. Benuel had complimented Susannah after lunch every day. Had he just been flattering her? "I thought you liked Susannah's cooking."

"I don't *dislike* it. I just prefer my meals prepared

the traditional Amish way." Benuel lowered his voice and added, "But I understand why she tries to cut back on calories or makes low-fat versions of what other *weibsleit* make. The *Englisch meed* I knew did the same thing to keep their weight down. Amish or *Englisch*, I suppose all *weibsleit* want to look their best—especially when they're single and they think it will help them attract a *mann*."

Benuel's reply surprised Peter for two reasons. Firstly, he hadn't realized Susannah had been cutting back on calories. The lunches she made were so tasty, especially in comparison to the processed food his sister usually bought, that Peter honestly hadn't noticed any difference between her cooking and the traditional Amish meals his mother used to make.

Secondly, although he'd noticed Susannah's weight loss, he hadn't suspected it was because she'd deliberately been on some kind of diet. Although in hindsight, he supposed that was more probable than her having lost weight due to an illness. Peter respected it if she was trying to take better care of her health, but Benuel had implied her real reason for losing weight was to catch the eye of a suitor. As becoming as she was, Susannah had never demonstrated that kind of vanity when Peter was courting her and he couldn't imagine that she'd consider her physical appearance worthy of so much focus. Yes, she'd always looked tidy and well-groomed, as was customary, but she wasn't the kind of woman who primped and preened in front of a mirror. She was more likely to be concerned about her inner character than her outer image.

Furthermore, her supposed desire to lose weight didn't seem like the kind of subject she would have discussed with a male acquaintance. Although it was possible she'd mentioned it to one of the women in the district and it had gotten back to Benuel, his perspective seemed to reflect *his* emphasis on outward appearances, not Susannah's. *It will take time for him to shake off the influence of the* Englisch *culture*, Peter thought.

Rather than respond to Benuel's remark, he asked for his help aligning the new board in the casing. Benuel quickly took over the entire installation and Peter was admittedly impressed by his adroitness and attention to detail. *At least the* Englisch *had a positive influence on him in regard to his craftsmanship*, he thought. Peter's mind immediately jumped to Hannes back at the workshop and he silently prayed that they'd receive at least a few orders this week.

Fifteen minutes later, when everyone was squeezed around the table or standing at the counter to eat lunch, Hannah asked if Peter and Benuel had been able to repair the board on the staircase.

"*Jah*. Except we didn't repair it—we replaced it entirely," Benuel answered. "It was splintered pretty badly. I've seen horses do less damage kicking a fence down than what you did to that board, Dorcas."

"Me?" Dorcas asked. "*I* didn't break it."

"*Neh?*" He scanned the room. "Oh, it was Eva?"

Eva paused with her fork in midair and she shook her head. "I wasn't even here when it happened."

It was clear to Peter that Benuel had assumed either Dorcas or Eva had broken the step because they were overweight, but he silently prayed the assumption would be lost on both of them.

"*I* was the one who broke it," Hannah admitted.

"You? But you're so thin," Benuel said and any hope

Peter had that Dorcas and his sister wouldn't be embarrassed flew right out the window. Dorcas's cheeks
turned bright red and Eva dipped her head and wiped
her mouth with a napkin, as if she was trying to hide.
Peter knew she was near tears.

He was just about to say that the stairs were so old
and worn that a person much lighter than Hannah could
have broken the step, too, when she diplomatically replied, "Thin or not, I can be a real klutz. I was running
down the stairs really fast and I hit the last step a lot
harder than I intended."

"*Jah*, it's amazing how powerful a slender person
can be," Susannah chimed in. "When I first saw you,
Benuel, I thought, 'He's so lanky, how is he ever going
to lift those potato barrels into the buggy wagon?' Yet
you slung them around like they were made of cardboard. I guess that's one of many reasons it's better
not to make judgments or comments about someone
else's size."

Because her tone was so pleasant, Benuel probably
didn't know whether to feel insulted or complimented
by Susannah's remark and he didn't reply. Peter wasn't
quite sure how she'd intended it, either, until he saw her
wink at Eva, who had dropped her napkin back onto
her lap and smiled at Susannah.

As much as he appreciated how graciously Susannah had interceded, Peter was filled with nostalgia. Up
until just now, he'd either been too nervous about of-
fending her or too busy eating the meals she'd made at
the farm to really reminisce about the reasons he'd liked
her so much. The way she'd responded to Benuel demonstrated both her strength and her gentleness: she had
effectively set him straight, without tearing him down.

And it made Peter remember that he used to daydream about what a good mother she'd make one day.

She'll still make a gut mamm, *but not for* my kinner. The thought filled him with such remorse he could hardly finish his lunch and he didn't take any of the three types of desserts offered to him, either.

After everyone was done eating, he excused himself to go upstairs and tighten the doorknob on the linen closet. Because the women had finished preparing the meals for Elizabeth and cleaning her house faster than they expected, they were ready to depart as soon as they'd washed and dried the lunch dishes. As Peter was lacing his boots, Eva and Dorcas shuffled down the hall.

"I told Dorcas we can drop her off on the way home, Peter."

"Sure." He moved over to make room for Susannah, who had come to put her boots on, too.

"Is anyone giving you a ride?" Eva asked her.

"My *groossdaadi* was supposed to pick me up at three o'clock, but I don't want to hang around here until then. If I walk quickly, I can make it home before he leaves the *haus*."

"But it's pouring outside," Eva pointed out. "You should ride with us."

Peter winced, imagining how Marshall would react to him bringing Susannah home. He didn't want to tell her outright that she couldn't ride with them, but neither did he want to encourage her. He held his breath, hoping she'd decline his sister's offer.

"Oh, but Susannah enjoys exercising in the rain," Dorcas said. "She's been cooped up indoors all week, isn't that right, Susannah?"

Susannah looked so dejected that Peter decided he'd

rather risk Marshall's ire than allow her to think that she was unwelcome, or that he hadn't meant what he'd said about being neighborly toward her.

But just then, Benuel came around the corner from the opposite direction. He must have heard their entire conversation because he said, "Unlike Peter, I'm going in your direction, Susannah. We'll have to drop Emily off at the *Englishers'* first, but we should make it to your *haus* in plenty of time to prevent your *groossdaadi* from heading out to get you."

Susannah glanced at the mechanical clock on the shelf and nodded. "I think that might be a better idea than walking. *Denki*, Benuel."

"No prob," he replied, just like an *Englischer*. And for some reason, the thought of Benuel giving Susannah a ride home alone disturbed Peter more than anything Marshall could have said to him.

Chapter Six

Since it was an off Sunday, Susannah worshipped with her grandparents, Jacob and Conrad at home in the morning. Afterward, they ate a light lunch, comprised solely of leftovers, since Susannah didn't cook on the Sabbath unless it was absolutely necessary. Then, since the sky was bright and sunny and it was the last opportunity to go fishing before the season ended for the year, the boys took off for Little Loon Pond.

Susannah wasn't sorry to see them go, but she was sorry they were taking the buggy because it meant she couldn't travel to the phone shanty. She had hoped to place a call to the phone shanty nearest her home in Dover, where she could leave a voice-mail message asking Charity to send the recipes for vegetable lasagna and a few other meals she intended to make. Iddo and Almeda Stoll—New Hope's deacon and his wife—were arriving later in the afternoon to visit Susannah's grandparents, so it would have been the perfect opportunity for her to slip away by herself. But since the boys took the buggy, out of respect for her grandparents' wishes,

Susannah wouldn't insist on walking to the shanty by herself.

So after a light lunch, she put on a pot of water for tea and sat in the living room with Lydia while it heated. Marshall was napping in the large chair at the opposite end of the room, next to the woodstove. At least, Susannah assumed he was napping; it was possible he was just closing his eyes because he didn't feel like being included in the women's discussion. Susannah didn't blame him; she didn't feel much like talking, either. She had a slight headache—she blamed it on eating either too much salt or too much sugar the previous day—and after the water came to a boil and she served tea, she hoped to go outside for a walk around the farm.

"Is Dorcas going to stop by today?" Lydia asked her.

"That would be nice, but I kind of doubt she will." Susannah had noticed Dorcas had been subtly cool toward her for the duration of the work frolic. And there was no question that she hadn't wanted Susannah to ride home with her and Peter and Eva. But Susannah realized she was probably the one at fault for that; it couldn't have been pleasant for Dorcas to be in the middle of the tension between Susannah and Peter. Now that they'd come to a truce of sorts, maybe Dorcas wouldn't have to try so hard to make up for Susannah's sour attitude toward him. "I'll have to apologize."

"Ach? Did you *meed* have a falling out?"

Susannah had been so deep in thought that she hadn't realized she'd voiced herself aloud. "*Neh*, not exactly. We just haven't been quite as close as we were last summer or at *Grischtdaag*," Susannah admitted. "It's probably because so much time has passed since the last time we saw each other. Writing letters is different than interacting in person."

"*Jah.* And I imagine she has to adjust to seeing you so thin. She might be a bit envious."

"*Neh*, I don't think so. She has never expressed being dissatisfied with her weight." On the contrary, she had sometimes commented that she was grateful she had a few extra pounds on her frame because she believed her stature helped her lift and carry the heavy trays of food at the Millers' restaurant more easily than some of the thinner waitstaff.

"Well, her *mamm* has told me she's been cutting back on what she eats, but she hasn't had much success losing weight."

Now that Lydia mentioned it, perhaps Dorcas was unhappy about her size. Susannah realized that might have explained some of her remarks. *If she wants to lose weight, I'd be* hallich *to share my recipes*, Susannah thought. *And I'll encourage her however else I can.*

Switching the subject, Lydia commented, "It was nice of Benuel to bring you home yesterday."

"I wouldn't have accepted a ride from him, but I didn't want *Groossdaadi* to have to *kumme* get me since Benuel was already there," Susannah emphatically explained, just as she'd done yesterday afternoon when she'd returned from the Hiltys' house.

"You know, your *groossdaadi* thinks he's got a *gut* head on his shoulders." Lydia lowered her voice. "I was surprised last night when he told me Benuel is a lot more financially responsible than Peter is."

Since when did other people's finances become such an important issue to Groossdaadi? *And what makes him think Peter isn't financially responsible?* Susannah wondered. While she agreed that it was important for men and women to be good stewards of the resources God gave them, she didn't believe it was her place—or her grandparents' place—to comment about how someone else handled their money.

"Whether that's true or not, it seems like a private matter between Peter, his *familye* and *Gott*."

Her response must have sounded sanctimonious, because Lydia quickly defended her husband, and said, "Marshall wasn't gossiping—he was telling me by way of saying how *hallich* he is that you're interested in Benuel, not Peter. I think he was even more delighted than I was when Benuel brought you home yesterday."

"I am *not* interested in Benuel!" Susannah exclaimed loudly. The fact that her grandfather didn't even flinch proved to her he was, indeed, only pretending to be asleep.

Lydia chuckled. "It's okay, dear. Your *groossdaadi* and I won't let on that we know, especially not in front of the *buwe*. We don't want them to tease you or make it uncomfortable for you to be around Benuel at lunchtime."

"Excuse me. I hear the kettle whistling." Susannah was so galled by Lydia's refusal to accept what she was telling her that she had to flee the room to keep herself from responding in an inappropriate manner. After turning off the stove element, Susannah went into the bathroom and splashed water on her face and then she opened the window. Leaning her elbows on the windowsill, she closed her eyes and allowed the crisp breeze to dry her cheeks and chin as she tried to think of a respectful way to tell Lydia and her grandfather that she wished they wouldn't meddle in her life so much. While she was resting there, she heard the familiar sound of a horse pulling a buggy up the lane. *It's Iddo and Almeda! Now I can finally go out for a walk alone.*

She straightened her prayer *kapp* and then returned to the living room. "I heard a buggy," she announced and this time her grandfather opened his eyes. "I'll fix a tray and say hello to Iddo and Almeda, then I'm going to take a stroll around the farm."

Susannah rushed into the kitchen before Lydia could insist that she ought to join her and Almeda for a visit instead of going outdoors. She pulled a plate from the cupboard and arranged several whoopie pies on it, as well as an assortment of cookies.

There were so many leftover desserts from yesterday's frolic that Faith had insisted she take home a bunch of goodies. "Since you don't eat desserts anymore, I suppose you don't bake them very often, either. But your household shouldn't have to suffer just because you're on a diet," she'd joked.

Conrad and Jacob had already polished off almost half of the sweets she'd brought home and Susannah hoped her grandparents, Almeda and Iddo would eat the rest this afternoon. Otherwise, Susannah might be tempted to overindulge. As she put teacups on the tray, Lydia shuffled through the kitchen with Marshall close behind.

"It's such a pleasant day that we're going to visit out on the porch," she told Susannah.

That's what I've been trying to get you to do all week, Susannah thought ruefully. She didn't understand her stepgrandmother's behavior lately. "I'll be right out with these treats."

When they got to the door, Lydia halted, almost as if

there was an invisible barrier keeping her from going any farther. Marshall reached to hold the door open for her with one hand, and with the other, he assisted her down the little ledge and onto the porch. Susannah had to admit to herself that her grandfather's watchfulness over his wife was rather sweet, even if she personally found it stifling for herself.

A minute later, she used her elbow to push open the door as she carried a tray outside. To her chagrin, it was Benuel, not Iddo and Almeda, who was conversing with her grandparents. "What are you doing here?" she asked without even saying hello. She set down the tray on the end of the bench next to the porch swing where her grandparents were seated.

Benuel held up a nine-by-thirteen-inch baking pan. "You left this in my buggy yesterday and I thought I'd better return it to you in case you needed it for breakfast."

Susannah had never heard such an implausible excuse in her life. She noticed even Lydia had turned her head sideways—was she trying not to laugh? "It's not mine. It must have been a pan Emily brought from your *ant*'s kitchen."

"Oh. Right. I should have asked her first."

"It was thoughtful of you to *kumme* all this way, Benuel," Lydia said, smiling. "Why don't you join us for a snack? We're waiting for Almeda and Iddo to arrive."

"Denki." Benuel stepped forward to take a seat on the bench, but when Susannah didn't move, he motioned to it and said, "After you, Susannah."

"Neh, I don't want to sit. I want to take a walk."

"That sounds *wunderbaar*," Benuel replied, nodding

as if she'd invited him to come, too. "Where do you want to go?"

Even without looking at Lydia, Susannah could feel the older woman's eyes on her and she knew she'd never hear the end of it if she told Benuel flat out that she didn't want him to come with her. She was about to say she'd changed her mind—that she'd prefer to stay there with her grandparents, the deacon and his wife. But then she realized Iddo and Almeda might get the wrong idea. Most, but not all, young Amish couples tried to keep their courtships a private matter, but a few made no concerted effort to hide their involvement with each other. And it wouldn't have been a stretch for the deacon and his wife to assume Benuel was at the house for the same reason Lydia had assumed he'd given Susannah a ride home.

Cornered, she was about to give in and allow him to saunter around the farm with her when she realized she could use this situation to her advantage. "I was just going to take a walk around the farm. But now that you're here, I wonder if you'd give me a ride to the phone shanty? Conrad and Jacob have taken the buggy and I need to call my sister-in-law."

Susannah would have been hard-pressed to determine who appeared most pleased by her suggestion: Marshall, Lydia or Benuel.

"Of course I will," Benuel said and practically danced down the porch steps.

"Don't hurry right back for my sake," Lydia called as Susannah reluctantly plodded after him. "If it gets late, Almeda can help me put supper on the table."

"We're only going to the phone shanty so I can leave a message for Charity. This isn't a leisurely outing,"

Susannah stated pointedly, so there'd be no question in anyone's mind about why she'd suggested Benuel give her a ride. But when she turned to wave goodbye, Lydia winked at her and held a finger to her lips, signifying she wouldn't disclose Susannah's "secret."

Unfortunately, Benuel didn't seem to take her at her word, either. "Since you wanted to go for a stroll, we could take a walk around Little Loon Pond after we go to the shanty," Benuel suggested as they headed toward the main road.

"Neh." As much as she loved the trail around the pond, Susannah didn't want to run in to Jacob and Conrad when she was out with Benuel, or else they might think he was courting her, too. Not to mention, Benuel might have interpreted her acceptance of the invitation as an encouraging sign. "As I told Lydia, my only purpose in going out is to make my phone call and then return home."

"Okay. But it sure is a beautiful day."

Susannah couldn't argue with him about that; the day was unseasonably warm. Peak fall foliage viewing for the elms, oaks and maples wouldn't happen for a few weeks, but the trees' colors were beginning to change and they provided a striking contrast with the abundant eastern white pines.

Since Susannah figured not even Benuel could misconstrue her comments about the weather or landscape as flirtation, she described the similarities and differences between this part of Maine with Dover. In turn, he told her about where he lived, too.

"There are some rigorous hiking trails leading up to the ridge, but the view of the lake from up there is well worth the effort. It's incredible," he raved. "There's a trail here in New Hope that's comparable—it goes through the gorge and up to Pleasant Peak."

"*Jah*. I know. I've hiked it several times." Technically, Susannah hadn't really *hiked* the trail. It was more like she and Peter used to amble through the woods in the same area, looking for a private, shady spot to picnic during the summer they'd courted.

One time they'd become so distracted talking to each other that they'd lost their way back to the parking lot. As they were trying to get their bearings, Peter had taken her hand in his for the first time. He'd apologized that the pads of his hands were calloused and his skin was rough from his work as a carpenter, but Susannah wouldn't have noticed; she was too giddy from the sensation of having her fingers intertwined with a man's for the first time in her life. *And for the last time*, she thought, quickly dismissing the memory.

"This is close enough," she said a minute later, hopping out of the buggy before it even rolled to a stop near the shanty. She didn't know why, but she didn't want Benuel to overhear the message she left for Charity. "I'll only be a minute," she promised.

But when she got through to the voice-mail recording for the phone in the shanty closest to her home in Dover, Susannah left a long, rambling message for her family. She hadn't realized how homesick she was until then and even though she knew they couldn't hear her, she felt as if she was talking directly to them. She mentioned she was praying about her father's medical checkup and that she hoped her niece was done cutting her tooth by now and was sleeping better. When she hung up, she realized she'd forgotten to ask Charity for the recipes, so she had to redial. She was so preoccupied with leaving her second message that until she hung up she didn't realize someone else had come from the opposite direction and was standing nearby to use the phone.

It was Hannah Miller and Dorcas. They must have walked from Dorcas's house; Susannah hoped nothing had happened to her horse or buggy. "Hello," she said, greeting them warmly. "What are you two doing here?"

"The same thing you're doing, *lappich*. Using the phone," Dorcas retorted.

Trying not to take offense at her sarcasm, Susannah clarified, "I just meant that I hope nothing's wrong... I mean, because you walked all this way to use the phone instead of coming by buggy. Your horse is all right, isn't she?"

"Of course." Dorcas sounded indignant. "I may not like to walk in the rain, but that doesn't mean I'm lazy, you know."

"I wasn't implying you're lazy," Susannah said softly. Given how sensitive Dorcas was about a thoughtful, straightforward inquiry, she was becoming more convinced that Lydia was right about her being envious of Susannah's weight loss after all. Still, it hurt to be the object of her friend's jealousy. And Susannah felt a little disappointed that Dorcas hadn't invited her to be part of her Sabbath recreation. *Hannah gets to see her all the time at the restaurant, but I'm only here for a few weeks and we had planned to spend as much time together on the weekends as we could.* "I'm just surprised to see you, that's all."

"Ooh—I think I know *why* we caught you off guard!" Hannah excitedly gave Susannah's arm a squeeze. She whispered, "Is that Benuel I see waiting for you in the buggy over there?"

Susannah glanced over her shoulder. "*Jah*. He just stopped by the *haus* to return a pan he thought was mine. I wanted to *kumme* to the shanty to call my *familye*, but Jacob and Conrad had taken my *groossdaadi*'s buggy, so Benuel gave me a ride." Even to her own ears, Susannah's explanation sounded as far-fetched as Benuel's excuse had originally sounded.

"Don't worry," Hannah said out of the corner of her mouth as she waved animatedly at Benuel. "You can trust us. We won't tell anyone, will we, Dorcas?"

"There's nothing to tell," Susannah insisted.

"Hi, Hannah. Hi, Dawn," Benuel called.

Susannah inwardly cringed because he'd gotten Dorcas's name wrong *again*, although at least he was getting closer. She thought her friend would deliver a snide comeback, but Dorcas plastered a smile on her lips and lifted her hand in a cheerful wave.

"*Neh*, we won't tell anyone about you and Benuel," she belatedly agreed with Hannah before following her into the phone shanty. "Have *schpass*, wherever you're going."

But Susannah *didn't* have fun; she had a headache. And the only place she was going was back to her grandparents' house, where she read alone in her room with a cup of tea, the last two cookies and half a whoopie pie left on the plate she'd set out for the guests.

On Sunday evening, Eva served reheated leftover cabbage-patch stew that Faith had sent home with her from the frolic.

"This is *appenditlich*," Hannes said. "Who made it?"

"Susannah Peachy. Do you like it, too, *Mamm*?"

"It's *wunderbaar*. I'll have another serving, please." Dorothy extended her bowl so her daughter could re-fill it.

For the second evening in a row, their mother had joined them for supper instead of retreating to her room early. Peter didn't know how long this spurt of energy would last, but he was grateful that the Lord had pro-vided Dorothy a little more stamina than she usually had. Hannes and Eva seemed uplifted by their mother's health improvement, too. Eva was especially bubbly, re-peating anecdotes and gossip from the frolic that she'd already told them about yesterday.

"Did you know that Hannah Miller and Isaiah Wittmer are getting married in December?" she asked her mother in a secretive tone.

Most, although not all, Amish couples in their dis-trict tried to keep their courtships private from their friends and family members. If they decided to marry, the announcement of their upcoming weddings were "published" or announced in church sometime in Oc-tober. And then the weddings took place on Tuesdays or Thursdays in November and December. However, Hannah and Isaiah had been courting for a long time and there were few people in the district who weren't aware that this was the year they were finally getting married. But now that Eva was a teenager, she seemed more interested in discussing courtships and weddings than she had previously.

"I think you mentioned it yesterday," Dorothy re-plied. "Didn't you tell us that her *mamm* wanted to host the *hochzich* meal at their restaurant instead of at the *kurrich* or in their home?"

The majority of couples in other states got married in the brides' homes, since that's where the Amish met for worship. But because the New Hope district had constructed a church building for worship, some couples chose to hold their weddings there. However, no couple had ever considered getting married in a restaurant before, not even in an Amish one that was family-owned.

"*Jah.* Even though the *Ordnung* doesn't forbid it, Isaiah's *mamm* didn't want them to have their *hochzich* meals at the restaurant because it seemed too much like an *Englisch hochzich* reception."

"I can understand that," Dorothy remarked. "Although it's not as if Hannah and Isaiah intend to give the furniture away afterward."

Everyone chuckled at her comment, which was a reference to the *Englisch* picnic-table order Hannes had received on Saturday for a wealthy *Englisch* couple's wedding reception. The bride and groom had impulsively decided to get married outdoors at the end of October and they wanted brand-new picnic tables handcrafted just for the reception. The wood was to be inscribed with their names and the wedding date; afterward, they intended to give the tables to their guests as gifts, or donate them to local parks. In order to fill the order by the deadline, Peter would have to help his brother in the workshop in the evenings, but he was grateful for the way the Lord had provided for this need, too.

"I wish one of *you* would get married soon," Eva commented to her brothers. "Then we could have a wedding *and* I'd finally have a *schweschder.*"

"Peter will probably get married before I do since

he's older," Hannes told her. "Although he's got to be a suitor before he can become a husband."

Don't hold your breath, Peter thought dolefully.

"Maybe he's already courted someone. And maybe *I* know who it is," Eva taunted.

Dorothy curiously tipped her head, eyeing Peter, and Hannes stopped slurping his broth and asked, "You're someone's suitor? If we guess who it is, will you tell us if we're right?"

"*Neh*, because I'm not courting anyone." Peter felt his cheeks burn.

Despite his obvious discomfort, his sister persisted, "Even if you're not exactly courting her right now, you *want* to court her, don't you?"

Peter didn't know how she'd found out he used to be Susannah's suitor, but he couldn't afford to have any rumors that he was interested in her again getting back to Marshall. He scowled and ignored her, but Eva persisted.

Addressing Hannes, she hinted, "I can't tell you her name but I *can* tell you she was at the frol—"

"*Absatz*, Eva!" Peter demanded. Seeing his mother flinch and his sister's eyes fill, Peter immediately regretted barking at Eva, especially because it was so rare for all of them to be engaged in such lively supper conversation. He rubbed his temples in slow circles and exhaled heavily. "I'm sorry," he apologized.

"That's okay, *suh*." His mother reached over and patted his arm. "You should go relax or read for a while. You seem tired."

"*Jah*. I think I'll hit the sack early tonight."

After he left the room, Peter heard Hannes as he scoffed, "Tired, nothing. Eva's right. Whether he's actually courting someone or not, he's got a *weibsmensch* on his mind."

As he got ready for bed, Peter mulled over his brother's comment. *I do* not *have a* weibsmensch *on my mind,* he silently argued. At least, not in the sense that Eva and Hannes were suggesting. Sure, over the weekend Peter had reflected on how relieved he was that he'd had a conciliatory chat with Susannah, but that wasn't the same thing as thinking about *her.* And, yes, he was looking forward to seeing her tomorrow, but only because he always got so hungry working on the farm and she was such a good cook.

Besides, even if he *had* entertained a fleeting notion about becoming her suitor again, Peter knew that a courtship with her was an impossibility. *Marshall would never allow it and Susannah would never want it,* he reminded himself. *Especially not if he told her why I broke up with her.* So as he lay down to go to sleep, he resolved to squelch any unprompted thoughts of romance as soon as they popped into his mind.

Chapter Seven

On Monday morning, Susannah woke with a stomachache. *Why did I eat supper last night?* she asked herself. *I was already full from the treats I had with my tea.* She'd only been in New Hope a little over a week and it seemed like the healthy habits she'd spent the past eight or nine months developing were melting away like whipped cream on warm apple pie…which she'd also eaten last evening, since Almeda had brought them two. No wonder her skirt felt tight.

Lord, please help me to exercise more self-control today, she prayed as soon as she'd gotten dressed, brushed her hair into a tight bun and pinned on her prayer *kapp.* Then she added, *And please help me to find a way to get together with Dorcas in private, so we can smooth things out between us.*

As she was making breakfast, Susannah mentally planned out her day. Like most Amish women, unless it was raining she considered Monday to be laundry day. Which didn't mean it was the only day they did laundry, but dirty clothes inevitably piled up over the weekend. Susannah intended to spend part of the morning running them through the ringer and then hanging them out to dry.

However, since she'd gone to the frolic on Saturday, she hadn't replenished their groceries for the first part of the week yet. *I guess I'll do that after lunch*, she decided. The thought of lunch put a smile on her face; maybe now that she wasn't at odds with Peter, she could relax and she wouldn't overeat. Perhaps she'd even enjoy conversing with him a little.

"Guder mariye," her grandfather said as he and Lydia came into the kitchen, where she'd just set a pan of meatless breakfast scramble on the table.

"You seem *hallich*. What are you thinking about?" Lydia questioned. "Or *who* are you thinking about that's lighting up your eyes like that?"

For a moment, Susannah felt as if her stepgrandmother had read the thoughts she'd just had about Peter. But then she realized she'd been referring to Benuel, so Susannah sighed. How was she going to convince Lydia she wasn't interested in him as a suitor?

"I'm just pleased it's sunny again today," she said as she poured coffee. "I need to go to the market. Would you like to ride with me?"

Lydia's countenance fell. *"Neh*. You go ahead without me. I'll just sit in the living room and read."

Her mewling reply grated on Susannah's nerves. Lydia had broken her wrist, not her ankle. Why was she acting as if she was almost completely incapacitated? "That's up to you, but I hope you don't expect me to hurry back," she snapped.

Lydia's eyes widened, but Susannah felt too cross to apologize. *I don't mind doing the housework and fetching her whatever she needs, but I'm tired of constantly*

entertaining her. She's acting as if she can't function un-
less I'm in the same room and I feel like I'm suffocating!

Susannah turned her back to arrange half a dozen
slices of bacon on a pan in preparation for broiling it,
which was somewhat healthier than frying. By the time
it was thoroughly cooked, both of the boys had come
in from doing the milking and everyone sat down to
eat. Susannah's grandfather seemed more talkative
than usual, perhaps because he was making up for the
strained silence between Susannah and Lydia.

"On *Dunnerschdaag*, Lydia and I are going to her
dokder's appointment," he informed Conrad and Jacob.
Because Lydia had suffered a severe compound frac-
ture, the specialist needed to take follow-up images to
confirm it was healing properly. If it wasn't, she'd possibly need surgery. "We'll be leaving at eleven o'clock
and not coming home until after supper, since we're
stopping to visit Lydia's *schweschder* in Serenity Ridge
on the way back. I'll have to make sure everyone knows
how to operate the digger, so someone can take my
place. The rest of you will need to pick and take turns
helping load the barrels onto the wagon. There's supposed to be rain coming on *Freidaag* or *Samschdaag*
again, so you're going to have to keep up the pace.
Keep your breaks to a minimum. Nothing longer than
five minutes."

Jacob nodded his agreement as he continued down-
ing his breakfast, but Conrad asked, "We only have five
minutes to eat lunch?"

"Don't be *lecherich*. Of course you'll take a full
lunch break," Lydia insisted. "Susannah will fix you
something, as usual."

"Aren't I going with you to the *dokder*?" Susannah

asked. She had assumed Lydia would want her to travel with them, since she might need someone to help her with doors in the women's room or something.

"*Neh.* The driver charges per passenger and besides, the *menner* will be *hungerich.* They can't harvest potatoes on empty stomachs. We'll be gone for most of the afternoon, so you'll need to stay home to get supper started, too."

Susannah could hardly contain her glee. *I'll have half a day all to myself*—and *I'll have the buggy to myself, too! After lunch, I can go talk to Dorcas, since she said she's not working until* Freidaag. *Maybe we can even take a walk at the gorge.* Susannah was so invigorated by the prospect that she whipped through her morning chores.

After hanging out the laundry, she came in to make up a grocery list, a task she and Lydia usually did together. But her stepgrandmother wasn't sitting in her usual chair, nor was she in the bathroom. Susannah went down the hall and gently tapped on the bedroom door. "Lydia? Are you okay?"

"*Jah,*" she answered tersely.

"I'm going to make up a grocery list before I fix lunch. Do you want to help me decide what we need?"

"*Neh.* You go ahead. Whatever you buy is fine, since you're the one doing all the cooking, anyway." Lydia still didn't come to the door.

Susannah hesitated. It was difficult holding a conversation this way, but she had an inkling Lydia was angry with her, so she asked through the wood, "Are you sure you don't want to help me?"

"*Jah.* I'd just appreciate having a little time to myself."

Not half as much as I'd *appreciate it*, Susannah thought, offended. She returned to the kitchen and checked the fridge and pantry to determine what items she'd need to restock. After making her list, she prepared lunch. When Conrad had asked at breakfast what she'd be serving for the noon meal, she'd told him they'd have French fries and fried chicken. But the fries were actually baked potato wedges and the chicken, which was coated with corn flakes, was also baked. She'd also serve steamed broccoli and salad, with a slice of leftover apple pie for dessert.

Although she thought she'd appreciate preparing the meal without Lydia sitting at the table talking the entire time, the more time that passed, the guiltier she felt. Whether Lydia had retreated to her room because she was annoyed with Susannah or not, she knew she owed her stepgrandmother an apology for having spoken so sharply to her. So after she'd put the meal in the oven and had set the table, she knocked on Lydia's door again.

Entering, Susannah found Lydia seated in the rocker near the window, an open Bible on her lap. She went over and sat on the edge of the bed. "I'm sorry I snapped at you earlier, Lydia."

Her stepgrandmother patted her knee. "I understand. You've been very patient with me and my demands. It must be difficult for you to take care of your old *groosseldre*, keep *haus* and make meals for everybody without anyone else to help you."

"*Neh*, it's not. I'm used to doing far more work at home. But even if I weren't, I *like* helping you however I can." Susannah chose her words carefully, trying to be kind yet direct at the same time. "I guess I'm used to being…a little more active."

"I'm being overbearing, aren't I?" She appeared so sorrowful that Susannah immediately consoled her.

"Not *overbearing*, it's just that… Well, *you're* usually more active, too, Lydia. I know there are a lot of things you can't do because of your wrist, but it's not like you to sit inside all day."

"*Jah.* You're right." She sighed, then confided, "I didn't tell you or Marshall this, but the evening we went out for milkshakes, I accidentally smacked my hand against the trash receptacle in the women's room and it hurt all weekend. Ever since then, I've been worried if I move around too much, I might fall again or do something careless and injure my wrist even worse. And the *dokder* said if it doesn't heal properly, they may have to put screws or a plate in it. I can't imagine having metal in my body. I'd feel like I was a piece of your *groossdaadi*'s farm equipment."

Although Lydia chuckled, Susannah's eyes welled with contrition. She couldn't believe that this whole time when her stepgrandmother had been sticking so close to her and wanting to sit down together all the time, it was because she was *afraid.* Susannah thought, *That's probably why she waited for* Groossdaadi *to help her out onto the porch yesterday, too. But at least he was sensitive about it, not impatient and snappish, like I was.* This morning she'd asked the Lord to help her exercise self-control about what food she'd put *into* her mouth, when she should have been more concerned about exercising self-control about the words that came *out of* her mouth.

"I'm sorry, Lydia. I didn't realize you were so worried about getting hurt again."

"I should have told you, but I didn't want to admit my fear because I felt like I wasn't trusting *Gott* enough."

"I'm *hallich* you told me. And I'm sorry for being impatient."

"I'm sorry I've kept you holed up indoors all week, listening to me nattering on and on. But I understand that a young *weibsmensch* needs to get out for a little *schpass* with her friends. Why do you think I'm so eager for Benuel to court you?"

Susannah chuckled. "I appreciate that, Lydia. But I'm honestly not interested in having Benuel as my suitor."

"Is it because you don't want a long-distance courtship?"

"*Neh*. It's because I don't want a courtship, period."

"You mean with Benuel...or with anyone?"

"With *any*one." Susannah didn't know how to make it any clearer than that.

"Why not? Don't you want to get married?"

Not unless I were to marry a mann *who'd love me for who I am, inside and out, no matter what. And I don't think a* mann *like that exists*, Susannah thought, but she answered lightheartedly, "*Neh*, because then I wouldn't be as free to *kumme* visit you and *Groossdaadi* whenever I want... And I really do love spending time with you." It was true; now that she'd had this heart-to-heart chat with Lydia, her resentment lifted and she treasured the opportunity to be in her grandparents' presence again.

"We love having you here, too... But I know two young *menner* who are going to be heartbroken to find out you're not interested in a suitor at all."

"*Two?*"

"*Jah*. Benuel and Peter."

Susannah guffawed. "I've already made it very clear to Benuel that I'm not interested in being courted by him, so if he's heartbroken, that's his own fault. And I'm absolutely positive that Peter has no interest in me."

"Trust me. I've seen how those two look at you. They're both smitten."

"*Neh.* They're just *hungerich*—they're smitten with the meals I make." Lydia's observation had caused Susannah to blush so she hopped to her feet to leave the room. "Speaking of lunch, the *hinkel* should be nearly done by now."

But when they went into the hall, Susannah could smell an acrid stench. The chicken and potato wedges weren't just done; they were burned to a crisp. After pulling the blackened food from the oven, she opened the windows to air out the room. That's when she noticed the broccoli she'd intended to steam was still in the colander in the sink. The men would be coming in any second now, so she decided to just serve it raw.

"The potatoes are unsalvageable," she admitted to Lydia as she disposed of them. "But I made a big salad and I think the chicken might be okay if we scrape the coating off."

"Do you need me to get a hose?" Conrad asked when he came through the door as she was talking.

"A hose? For what?" Susannah absently replied, peeking into the bread box; there was only a quarter of a loaf left, but they were so low on groceries they'd just have to make do with what they had.

"To put out whatever is on fire."

"*Voll schpass,*" she retorted and turned around to make a face at him, as they sometimes did in jest.

But Conrad had walked down the hall and Peter was

alone on the braided rug by the door, wiping his feet. When he saw her, he grinned and said hello, his eyes twinkling. Lydia's comment instantly flashed through Susannah's mind. Was she right; did Peter look at her as if he was smitten? *Neh. He's just amused because he caught me making a* lappich *expression*, she rationalized. As for the topsy-turvy way *she* felt, that was just because she was heady from the fumes of the burned food.

Yet a few minutes later, when they were seated at the table and their elbows bumped as they folded their hands to say grace, a tingling sensation buzzed up her arm and across her shoulders, making her shiver.

"Are you cold?" Benuel asked. Sometimes she felt like he was observing her as closely as Lydia had been for the last week.

"A little," she told him, so he immediately offered to close the windows for her.

"*Neh*, that's okay. I'd rather be cold than tolerate that *schtinke*." Lifting the lid off the serving dish she'd put the chicken in, she announced, "I'm sorry, everyone, but as you can see, I burned the main dish. But there's plenty of salad and half a slice of bread apiece. I set this *hinkel* out in case someone is brave enough to try it, but it's probably not edible."

"It's fine," Benuel contradicted, jabbing a fork into the biggest piece of chicken on the platter. "It's just a little brown."

Susannah noticed Lydia was smirking, just as she'd done yesterday when Benuel claimed he'd come to the house to return the pan, but fortunately, she didn't say anything aloud.

However, Conrad jeered, "If that *hinkel* looks a little brown to you, you need glasses, *mann*. Because that stuff is as black as sin."

But Benuel persevered, sawing into the chicken with a knife and then lifting the bite-size piece to his lips. *He didn't even scrape off the charred part*, Susannah thought, glancing at him from the corner of her eye. *What is he trying to prove?*

Peter must have been thinking the same thing, because before Benuel put the chicken in his mouth, he interrupted him as he remarked, "I thought you said you've done a lot of carpentry work, Benuel."

"I have. Over five years' worth."

"Then you should know you'd better sand that chicken down before you eat it," he mocked.

There was a half-second pause and then Susannah burst out laughing and so did the others. Even Marshall chuckled. Benuel set down his fork in defeat and Susannah got up and whisked the dish of burned chicken off the table.

"I shouldn't have even set this out. While you're eating your salad, I'll make scrambled *oier* to fill you up. It will only take a few minutes." Lifting a skillet from the bottom cupboard, she added brightly, "And we'll have apple pie for dessert."

"*You're* serving dessert at lunchtime?" Jacob teased. "Is it a special occasion?"

"*Neh*, there's no special occasion," Susannah replied, as she turned to smile at everyone. "Just special people."

Peter felt like Susannah was speaking only to him. Or was it that he *wanted* her to be speaking only to him? Was he already entertaining the very kinds of romantic thoughts he'd just resolved to put out of his mind the evening before?

No, he didn't think so. It was probably more that he just didn't want Susannah to consider *Benuel* special in a romantic sense. Not because Peter had any hope of courting her, but because Benuel was obviously trying to win her over with insincere flattery. She deserved someone more straightforward than that. *She deserves someone more straightforward than* I *was, too,* he reminded himself. Benuel's dishonesty about how he regarded her cooking paled in comparison with how Peter hadn't been forthcoming about the reason he'd broken up with her.

"I'll be away from the *bauerei* on *Dunnerschdaag* afternoon," Marshall mentioned as they were waiting for Susannah to finish scrambling the eggs. "So I'll need to make sure you all know how to gauge the digger point."

When Peter was a teenager, he'd helped Amos, Marshall's brother, during three consecutive harvest seasons, so he was aware that if the blade went too deep, it would slice into the potatoes, ruining them. He considered it a cinch to operate a mechanical digger, but Jacob, Conrad and Benuel had never harvested potatoes before, so it was understandable they'd need to receive Marshall's instruction.

"Who's going to be digging?" Benuel asked.

"I don't know. We'll have to see how each of you handles the equipment first."

Susannah placed two bowls of eggs at each end of the table, then prepared to take her seat again. Benuel was crowding her on her left side and as she sat down, she wobbled toward Peter, but caught her balance by placing her palm on his shoulder. It only took a second for her to steady herself and withdraw her hand, but her momentary touch warmed Peter from head to toe.

He dared not look anywhere except at his plate until the feeling passed. The problem was, it *didn't* pass, not even when he noticed out of the corner of his eye that Marshall was glaring at him. It was as if he thought Peter were the one who'd grasped Susannah's shoulder, instead of the other way around. His mouth went dry, making it difficult for him to swallow his food, and he'd only taken two bites of pie by the time everyone else had finished their dessert.

"Time to get back to work," Marshall ordered and the other men pushed their chairs back and started filing out the door.

"But, *Groossdaadi*, Peter's not done with his pie yet," Susannah pointed out. "And that's practically the main course of this meal."

Marshall glowered, but as he put his hat on, he told Peter, "We'll be in the north field."

"I'll be right out," Peter said, shoveling another bite into his mouth and triggering a coughing spasm.

"Take your time," Lydia told him once Marshall exited the house. "Sweet things are meant to be savored."

Susannah was still seated beside him and Peter thought he noticed her shake her head at her stepgrandmother, but maybe he'd imagined it. "This does taste *gut*," he agreed.

"*Jah*. But it's not as *gut* as the pies your *mamm* used to make," Susannah commented. "I mean, I really appreciate that Almeda made pies for us. But your *mamm*'s were extraordinarily *appenditlich*. Especially her *blohbier* pies."

"*Jah*. I remember that time you traded me your entire

lunch for a second piece of her pie." Peter hadn't considered what he was disclosing until Susannah knocked her knee against his beneath the table. It was too late: Lydia's ears had already perked up.

"When was that?" she asked.

"It was on a *Sunndaag* last summer when some of us went on a picnic after *kurrich*," Susannah immediately said. Which was true, although "some of us" really meant "the two of us." Peter and Susannah never picnicked with anyone else when they were courting; Sundays were the only chance they had to be alone. They'd find a way to sneak to the gorge, which wasn't easy considering Susannah's grandparents didn't like her to walk anywhere on her own and she seldom had use of the buggy. Dorcas, the only person they told about their courtship, frequently dropped off Susannah at the gorge, where Peter would be waiting for her.

"Ah, that's right. You and Dorcas loved going out to the gorge on *Sunndaag*," Lydia recalled. "I didn't realize you'd gone with a group."

Susannah started coughing into her napkin. Or was she trying not to laugh? Peter couldn't tell. *How could I have been so* dumb *as to blurt out something like that?* he lamented. He wasn't particularly worried that Lydia would discover they'd been courting—for all Peter knew, Marshall had already told her. But he was worried what Susannah thought about him openly reminiscing about picnicking with her in the past.

After Lydia rose, put her plate in the sink and then excused herself to the restroom, Peter mumbled quietly to Susannah, "Sorry about that. It just slipped out."

"It's okay. Sometimes things spring to my mind, too, and I say them without really thinking them through."

It felt strange to be sitting side by side with her, with no one else on the other side of the table. No one else in the room. It reminded Peter of when they'd sit on a rock by the creek in the gorge, dangling their feet into the water and chatting as they ate their sandwiches. And instead of pushing the romantic memory from his mind, Peter deliberately indulged it, lingering over his pie even though he knew Marshall would have something to say about his delay when he returned to the fields.

Susannah didn't seem in any hurry to get up, either. She was silent while he whittled his pie down to the last two bites. Then she asked, "How is your *mamm*? At the frolic, someone mentioned she's been…under the weather."

I'm sure they did, Peter thought and instantly the nostalgic connection he felt with Susannah was replaced by insecurity about whatever rumors she'd heard about his mother. Peter could bear it if Marshall thought ill of him, but he didn't want Susannah to think his mother was lazy. "She's okay," he said and abruptly stood up, even as he was scooping the last bite of pie into his mouth. "I'd better get going or your *groossdaddi* won't let me take any more lunch breaks after this."

He'd only been half-joking about Marshall, but Susannah replied, "Don't worry, Lydia would never let that happen." Standing, she caught his eye and added, "And neither would I."

Peering into her earnest golden-brown eyes, Peter was overcome with affection. *"Denki,"* he said and then forced himself to leave the house while his legs could still carry him out to the fields.

I can't believe he still remembers that time I exchanged my lunch for his pie, Susannah thought as she began gathering the dirty dishes. But what struck her even more was the fondness she'd noticed in his voice as he recalled the memory.

Then her thoughts jumped to the remark Peter had made to Benuel about sanding down his chicken, and she laughed aloud. One of the things she'd always appreciated about Peter was that when he said he liked something, she could trust he was telling the truth, not just saying what she wanted to hear. Unlike Benuel, whose compliments seemed insincere and excessive. *How could* Groossdaadi *and Lydia think I'd ever choose Benuel over Peter?* she wondered. Not that she'd ever accept Peter as a suitor again, either. But even as a friend, she definitely preferred Peter's company over Benuel's.

When she had cleaned, dried and put away the lunch dishes, Susannah got ready to go to the market for groceries. "Are you sure you don't want to *kumme*?" she asked Lydia. "I can help you get in and out of the buggy. We'll be very careful."

"*Denki*, but I'd prefer to stay home. I might actually take a walk to the mailbox in a few minutes."

Pleased that Lydia felt confident enough to go for a stroll by herself, Susannah happily set out for the market. Upon arrival, she hitched the horse in an area of the lot specifically designated for buggies, right next to another Amish buggy. She was almost at the entrance to the store when she spotted Dorcas coming out, pushing a cart filled with groceries.

"Look who's here," she exclaimed. "Hi, Dorcas."

Dorcas squinted against the sun. "Oh. Hi, Susannah," she replied flatly.

"I'm *hallich* we're bumping into each other. There's something I'd like to chat with you about."

"Okay, but you'll have to talk while I'm loading these into the buggy. I don't want to be late picking my *schweschdere* up from *schul*."

So Susannah followed her to the buggy and helped her place the groceries into the back of the carriage. As they were carrying out the task, she asked, "Would you like to go on a hike to the gorge on Thursday afternoon? I can pick you up, since I'll have use of the buggy that day."

"*Neh*, I don't think so, but *denki* for asking."

Susannah waited, expecting her friend to explain why she couldn't go hiking, but Dorcas just turned and rolled her empty cart to the trolley. Feeling slighted, Susannah waited for her to return and then she asked, "Is something wrong? I feel like there's tension between us and I don't know if I've done something to upset you."

Dorcas pushed her prayer *kapp* strings over her shoulders. "I just don't consider going hiking to be as much *schpass* as you do."

"Then we don't have to hike. I only suggested that because—"

"Because you like lots of outdoor activity and Lydia has been keeping you cooped up in the *haus* all week. I know—you already told me," Dorcas said. "But *I* get lots of outdoor activity. Every *Sunndaag* I take a long walk. The rest of the week I'm outside doing yard work and caring for the animals and making sure my little *brieder* don't get hurt when they're running around all over the place. And when I'm not watching them or helping my *mamm*, I'm on my feet at the restaurant. So if *you* need more exercise, you should ask your suitor to take you hiking."

Susannah had no idea why Dorcas sounded so defensive, but she could no longer bridle her tongue. "What I was *going* to say before you interrupted me was that I only suggested a hike because I was looking forward to spending time chatting with you, the way we used to. It wouldn't have mattered to me if we climbed Mount Katahdin or just sat on the porch swing. I just wanted to be in your company." Susannah was so upset, her voice was shaking. "And as I've already told you, I'm not interested in being courted by Benuel. Or anyone else, for that matter."

"So you've mentioned." Dorcas snickered. "But you're doing a lot of riding around together for someone who claims she's not interested in him."

"I've ridden with him two times. Two! On *Samschdaag*, I rode with him because it was raining. And yesterday I needed to get to the shanty," Susannah explained again. "To suggest that I want him to be my suitor when I'm honestly telling you I don't is as *lecherich* as—as suggesting you and Peter are interested in each other because he gave *you* a ride home!"

"Why is that idea *lecherich*?" Dorcas's cheeks reddened. "Is it so unimaginable that someone would want to be my suitor?"

"*Neh*, of course it isn't." Susannah could see the pained look on her friend's face, so she lowered her volume. "I think almost any *mann* would be thrilled to court you. But based on my experience with Peter, I'm just not sure he's one of them." She reached to pat her friend's shoulder, but Dorcas jerked her arm away.

"I have to go pick up my *schweschdere*." She headed

toward the front of the buggy to unhitch the horse from the post. Coming around to the side when she was done, she glanced at Susannah and asked, "Did it ever occur to you that your weight wasn't the reason Peter broke up with you?" Then she climbed in without waiting for an answer.

Jah, it did, Susannah thought as Dorcas pulled out of the parking lot. Hundreds and hundreds of times. But if that wasn't the reason, then what was? *I can't start wondering about that again. I'll drive myself to distraction.* She briefly considered asking Peter about it directly. Now that so much time had passed and her emotions weren't running so high, maybe he'd be willing to offer her more of an explanation.

Neh, I'd better not do that, she decided as she wheeled a stray cart into the grocery store. *We've just gotten comfortable being around each other again. Knowing* why *Peter broke off our relationship won't change anything now, so it's better to leave the past behind.*

Chapter Eight

Tuesday morning seemed to arrive earlier than usual for Peter. He felt bleary-eyed as he journeyed toward the farm and reflected on the discussion he and Hannes had the evening before. They'd stayed up late planning the wedding picnic-table project in detail. They'd made a budget, determined what supplies they'd need to order, decided on a delivery company and wrote an estimate for the *Englisch* couple.

They'd taken on big orders before, but this one was challenging because the customers required octagonal tables, with angled attached benches. Because of the unique design of the table, the board lengths weren't standard, so Hannes was going to have to custom-cut them.

"So much for getting a head start on our next order," his brother had said in reference to the standard-shaped tables he'd been working on all week.

"It's not wasted effort," Peter had reminded him. "We don't want to turn down or delay any smaller orders that come in while we're working on this project, so it's *gut* you've increased our inventory."

"*Jah.* As it is, we're going to be hard-pressed to meet the deadline for the wedding."

"I'll help you in the evenings and on any day it rains. We'll get it done."

Now, as he directed his horse toward the farm, Peter wasn't feeling quite as confident about their ability to complete the order in time. The workshop had lights that were powered by a generator, so technically, the brothers could work as long as they needed to in the evenings. However, the work on the farm was grueling and Peter was exhausted by the time he got home.

Marshall really should have at least one additional person on the crew. And, ideally, he should have two or three, he thought. Once again, he wondered why Susannah wasn't helping pick potatoes, too, at least for some part of the day. Plenty of girls and women picked potatoes on *Englisch* and Amish farms alike. So it wasn't as if it was considered men's work by anyone's standards.

Out of the blue, it occurred to Peter that maybe Marshall wasn't relieving Susannah of any farm work responsibilities because he didn't want her doing such rigorous labor. *Maybe he's just trying to limit any interactions she might have with me.* If that was true, it seemed as if the old man was cutting off his nose to spite his face. *He's only making more work for himself and his crew*, he thought.

It was discouraging to suspect that Marshall thought so lowly of him that he'd rather risk not finishing harvesting before the first hard frost than to risk…what? Susannah *talking* to Peter in passing in the field when Marshall wasn't looking? *That's* lecherich*, especially since we sit inches apart from each other every day at lunch.* Of course, his invitation was at Lydia's insistence, so Marshall hadn't really had a choice. And maybe he felt as if nothing would develop between Peter and Susannah at the lunch table because he was right there to monitor every word Peter spoke to her.

However, he couldn't monitor every *thought* Peter had about her. Such as the one that ran through his mind later that afternoon when he entered the house and she turned from the oven to greet him. *I could go back outside right now without eating a single morsel and I'd still have enough energy to work for eight more hours, just because of her smile*, he thought.

Fortunately, he got to enjoy her smile *and* her cooking, a double blessing. After Marshall said grace, Conrad commented, "Oh, wow—beef Stroganoff. My favorite!"

"I'm *hallich* you like it," Susannah replied.

"You should hear him talking about your cooking," Benuel added. "He spends the entire morning wondering what's for lunch and then the entire afternoon guessing what's for supper."

Jacob joked, "He talks about food as much as Benuel talks about *weibsleit*. Especially about—"

Peter abruptly cut him off, and commented, "Sounds like you *menner* are doing a lot of talking when you should be working."

He knew it wasn't his place to admonish Jacob, but he hadn't wanted him to embarrass Susannah by announcing that Benuel frequently brought her up in conversation. He anticipated Marshall was going to be annoyed that Peter had usurped his position, but the old man simply said, "You're *all* doing a lot of talking when you should be eating."

So the group finished their meal in relative silence.

Afterward, when Marshall had gone into the bathroom, Lydia was standing in front of the sink as the other men were beginning their exodus out of the house, so Peter leaned over and whispered to Susannah. "Your *turkey* Stroganoff was *appenditlich*." He'd been able to taste that it wasn't beef and he actually preferred it the way she'd prepared it.

"Shh." She squeezed his forearm with one hand and put a finger to her lips with the other. "Don't tell anyone, okay?"

Just then, Marshall crossed the threshold into the room. Peter immediately lurched away from Susannah and toward the door, his heart pummeling his rib cage. But her grandfather clearly hadn't noticed that they'd been sharing a secret because he trailed Peter out to the fields without saying a word.

I've got to be more careful the next time I make a private comment to Susannah, he thought. And there *would* be a next time. Because he'd decided that no matter how hard Marshall had been trying to control what Peter said to her—and no matter how hard Peter had been trying to control his own thoughts *about* her—he wasn't going to stop trying to make Susannah smile.

Susannah couldn't help humming as she cleared the table; having a more harmonious relationship with Lydia and Peter again put a song in her heart. *Lord, please help Dorcas and me restore our friendship again, too*, she prayed. While she thought her friend's bitter attitude toward her was undeserved and the comments she'd made about Benuel and Peter were unfounded, she couldn't completely get them out of her mind.

Primarily, Dorcas's remarks made Susannah question whether she'd made it plain enough to Benuel that she wasn't interested in him romantically. *I've tried to communicate that to him, both indirectly and directly. I've ignored his flirting. I repeatedly said my purpose in riding with him on* Sunndaag *was so I could make a phone call. What else can I do?* she ruminated. It wasn't as if he'd actually asked to be her suitor yet. So it would have been vain and presumptuous to take him aside and say, "I want you to know I have no desire to be courted by you."

In addition to that dilemma, Susannah again found herself wondering if Dorcas herself hoped to start a courtship with Peter. She hadn't explicitly said that she did. But given that she'd claimed a woman usually only accepted a ride from a man if she was interested in him romantically, Susannah thought it was reasonable to infer Dorcas wanted Peter to be her suitor. Not only had she ridden with him twice, but her voice also became sugary sweet whenever she spoke to him.

The possibility that Dorcas was enamored with Peter troubled Susannah. And although she tried to tell herself it was because she didn't want Dorcas to get hurt the way she'd gotten hurt by him, in her heart Susannah knew that wasn't the only reason. It was also because if Peter *did* end up courting Dorcas, it would confirm that Susannah's weight had nothing to do with why Peter broke up with her. And it would indicate that he thought Dorcas was a better match for him than Susannah had been.

Dorcas wants a suitor and she wants to get married. So what is wrong with me that I wouldn't be hallich *for her—and for Peter—if it turned out they were* Gott's *intended for each other?* she asked herself. *It's not as if I'd want Peter as a suitor again...is it?* She wasn't so certain of the answer to that question any longer. But Susannah did know that she definitely wanted Dorcas for her friend and that they needed to resolve the tension between them.

She decided Thursday would still be a good day to seek her out, so she woke early that day to make a special treat to bring with her. Dorcas loved a dessert called funny cake, so-named because it was half pie and half cake. She also loved pumpkin pie. So Susannah made a funny cake that required pumpkin. Assuming Lydia was right about Dorcas trying to lose weight, Susannah reduced the amount of sugar and flour listed in the recipe. Since she had extra pumpkin, she used it to make muffins, which she added to the thermal bag she prepared for her grandparents to take on their excursion to the medical clinic.

"I put extra goodies in with your lunch in case your appointment runs long," she told her grandparents later as she walked them out to where the driver was idling his car.

"*Denki.* We should be home by around seven o'clock, but don't worry about us if we're not."

As Susannah watched Marshall help ease Lydia into the back seat, they both seemed so vulnerable to her that she silently prayed, *Please,* Gott, *watch over them on their trip. If it's Your will, give Lydia* gut *news about her wrist. And if the news is bad, give her grace and strength.*

After waving to them, she went back inside. The house felt oddly empty without Lydia in it, but Susannah didn't have time to dwell on any twinges of loneliness; she had to get busy making chicken-and-pepper fajitas for lunch. They weren't standard Amish fare and Susannah had never made them, but since her grandparents were away, she'd decided to give them a try. She wasn't sure the boys would like them, but she knew Peter would; the only time she'd ever eaten them was when he'd taken her out to a Mexican restaurant last summer.

Actually, it wasn't even a restaurant—it was a food truck that had parked in the lot by the large market. Peter had heard about how good the food they served was from Hannes, who'd been hanging out with a lot of *Englischers*.

Peter was probably relieved when his bruder *was baptized into the* kurrich *last spring,* she thought. *Hannes must have matured quite a bit since I knew him. Otherwise, Peter wouldn't be allowing him to manage the shop by himself.*

Suddenly, she remembered what Dorcas had said to her last week about how strange it was for Peter to be helping Marshall with the harvest. Susannah hadn't really thought twice about it, since she'd assumed he was just being a supportive community member. But now it struck her as odd that he'd put her grandfather's farm before his own business. Especially since yesterday, Peter had mentioned at lunch that the workshop had received a picnic-table order for an *Englisch* couple's wedding at the end of October.

I suppose he didn't count on his business picking up, she concluded. *I hope he doesn't regret offering to help* Groossdaadi, *though, because if he hadn't, we never would have become friendly to each other again.*

"What's that I smell?" Conrad asked after the men

had come in, washed their hands and gathered in the kitchen about an hour later.

"*Hinkel* fajitas with peppers."

"Trust me, you'll love it," Peter told him, taking his usual seat next to Susannah's chair.

"Where's my plate?" Benuel asked.

"Oh, I put it there, where Lydia usually sits. I figured this would give us both a little more elbow room." What Susannah had really figured was that this was another opportunity to indirectly demonstrate she wanted to keep distance between them.

"But you don't need more elbow room from Peter, eh?" Jacob asked, and she could feel her face flush with embarrassment. She hadn't thought about how it would look for her to move one of the men farther away from her, but not move the other.

Thinking quickly, she said, "You know how strongly my *groossdaadi* feels about being the head of his household and at the head of the table. I didn't think it was right to put Peter in his chair."

Her answer seemed to suffice and Jacob dropped the subject. As usual, once they'd said grace and were served, hardly anyone spoke because they were all too busy consuming their food. But after they'd had seconds and their eating slowed, Benuel told her how much they'd enjoyed the meal.

"*Es muy bueno,*" Peter added.

Susannah giggled. She silently recalled that the day they were waiting for their order at the food truck, the server had asked them how to say "It's very good" in *Deitsch.* Then she'd taught them how to say the same phrase in Spanish.

Benuel furrowed his eyebrows. He apparently didn't

enjoy the meal as much as he'd said he did, because he'd only eaten a single fajita. Even more telling, he'd taken two helpings of salad, which was unusual for him. "What did you say?" he asked Peter.

"Nada," Susannah answered for him. *Nada*, meaning *nothing*, was another word the server had taught them.

"Gut memory," Peter said, complimenting her.

It was such a fun day, I remember everything about it, she thought wistfully.

Peter didn't know if Benuel's nose was bent out of shape because he was annoyed that Peter was joking with Susannah, or if it was because he hadn't gotten enough to eat. But Benuel glowered at him as he said, "If you're done making jokes, we should get back to the field. I'll dig—the *buwe* can pick."

"It doesn't make sense for you to dig. That's a job for someone who isn't as strong as you are. You and I need to load and transport the barrels. Let Conrad or Jacob dig. The other *bu* can pick until it's time to load. Then we'll take turns transporting and unloading, as usual."

"Who did Marshall put in charge? Me or you?"

Marshall had told Benuel he expected him to keep an eye on everything, but the notion of being "in charge" was more of an *Englisch* one than an Amish one. They were all supposed to work together collaboratively. Furthermore, Peter knew more about harvesting potatoes than Benuel did. But he also knew he had to tread carefully, since Marshall held Benuel in high regard. "I'm just concerned about being one *mann* short today."

"If you need another person to pick, I can help after I do the dishes," Susannah volunteered.

Peter thought that was an even worse idea than

Benuel digging; he could imagine how upset Marshall would be. But Benuel was all for it. "*Jah.* That would be great. Like Peter said, Conrad and Jacob can take turns digging. Peter can do the loading and transporting, and the rest of us can pick."

How can he expect me to do all *the loading, transportation and unloading, just so he can be around Susannah?* Peter wondered, fuming inwardly. But he knew the more forcefully he resisted Benuel's instructions, the deeper Benuel would dig in his heels. So he offhandedly reminded him, "You know if one of us gets an injury, Marshall won't be able to finish harvesting on time, right?"

"*Jah.* So be careful out there." Benuel's scowl had been replaced with a grin.

Gott, please give me patience, Peter prayed as he headed out to the fields a few minutes later and began picking. Within half an hour, Susannah had come outside, too. Of course, Benuel suggested she work in the row next to him, while Peter and Conrad were picking in rows about fifty yards away. Jacob maneuvered the horse and digger, overturning the earth and bringing the potatoes to the surface.

Although Peter was too far away to hear what Benuel was saying, he could hear him jabbering to Susannah almost the entire time they were picking. On occasion, her voice could be heard briefly. After a while, Benuel's comments became less frequent and when Peter turned around, he understood why: Susannah had been picking so much quicker than Benuel that she'd moved up the row, too far away from Benuel for conversing. Peter grinned to himself. *I* knew *she wasn't lazy*, he thought.

In fact, a couple of hours later, when Benuel suggested it was time for another break, Susannah objected. "Already? We just took one."

"The *gaul* needs water and so do I," Benuel replied, and Jacob and Conrad agreed.

So did Peter. "*Jah*," he said. "I don't think we'll be able to fit any more barrels in the wagon. I should make a run to the potato *haus*."

"Okay, I know when I'm outnumbered." Susannah wiped her hands against her apron. As the five of them walked toward the barn, she asked, "Is anyone *hungerich* again?"

"*Jah*. Starving." Conrad was the first to reply, of course, but the other men quickly echoed his sentiment. So Susannah said she'd bring a treat out to them. After they'd walked out of the fields, she headed in the direction of the house while the men headed toward the barn. Peter was alarmed to see Hannes's buggy and horse hitched to the post and Hannes was heading in his direction.

Peter immediately suspected their mother was ill. But he waited until Hannes had greeted the other men and they'd gone into the barn, then asked, "What's wrong?"

"Nothing. I just need your signature on a few things for the project." Since Hannes wasn't eighteen yet, Peter had to sign off on all their legal documents, including purchase orders. "I wanted to put in the order for the wood today so it'll be delivered by *Samschdaag*. Eva needed me to take her to the grocery store, so I picked her up from *schul* on my way."

Peter glanced at the empty buggy. "Where is she?"

"She went up to the *haus* to say hello to Lydia and Susannah."

"Oh." Peter reviewed the paperwork to be sure his brother's figures were correct. Then Hannes handed him a pen and he signed it. "If you want to bring this to the lumber yard before it closes, you'd better go see what's keeping Eva." Peter always got a little nervous about what Eva might say to other women once she got chatting.

Just as he finished his sentence, he spotted Eva coming out of the house carrying a pitcher and some paper cups. Susannah was behind her with a basket.

"Hi, Hannes," she greeted his brother when she was within earshot. Her face was dirt-streaked and her hair was "poofing up," as she used to say about it, but she had a bright, warm smile. "Would you like a muffin and cider?"

So Eva and Hannes joined the others as they stood around the entrance of the barn, eating their snack. Peter noticed his sister seemed more reticent than usual and he wondered if her shyness had anything to do with meeting two new boys her age. She was such a smart, pretty and earnest young girl and Peter knew it wouldn't be long before she'd want to have a suitor. *But right now, she's far too young*, he thought. Fortunately, Jacob and Conrad seemed to be paying more attention to their muffins than to her.

"We'd better get going," Hannes urged Eva as soon as he'd finished eating. "I want to get to the lumber yard by four thirty."

Eva quickly popped the rest of her muffin into her mouth. Before leaving, she said to Susannah, "I'll see you on *Samschdaag*."

Peter's heart skipped a beat. "What happens on *Samschdaag*?"

"If Lydia doesn't mind being alone, Susannah wants to *kumme* visit *Mamm*." Eva's face was aglow. "And she's going to teach me to make one of her favorite recipes. Isn't that nice?"

Nice? It's baremlich*! When Marshall finds out, he's going to think this was* my *idea*, Peter worried to himself. *And who knows what Susannah's going to think when she sees* Mamm.

After saying goodbye to Hannes and Eva, Susannah realized there wouldn't be time for her to visit Dorcas after all; besides, she'd rather keep picking potatoes. Although her lower back was sore, she felt revitalized by the fresh air and hard work. Because she needed to use the restroom before returning to the fields, she started back toward the house with the tray and basket. Peter tramped toward the buggy wagon, while the men went back into the barn to fill a bucket for the horse and try to find the oil to grease the bearing components of the digger. She had gotten halfway to the house when she remembered to check the mail to see if Charity had sent her the recipes she'd requested, so she turned around.

Peter must have forgotten something, too, because she saw him heading back to the barn. Head down, he ducked inside the open barn door just as she approached it a few yards behind him. She was planning to tell the young men it would be a few more minutes before she joined them when she heard Benuel's teasing words. "I saw you eyeing Peter's *schweschder*, Conrad."

"If you did, it's only because I never saw a *maedel* eat anything so fast," Conrad replied, causing someone—Benuel? Jacob?—to laugh. "If she keeps that up, she'll wind up as big as Susannah used to be."

Susannah stopped cold in her tracks, a bilious taste rising in her mouth. She wanted to flee, but her legs felt as stiff and heavy as iron. Even though she hadn't reached the door yet and she couldn't see where anyone inside was standing, it was obvious to Susannah that none of the other men knew Peter had entered the barn. She was close enough to hear him loudly clear his throat.

"Er, sorry. I was just—" Conrad began, but Peter finished his sentence for him.

"You were just being unkind and ungodly, that's what you were doing." Peter's voice was deep and angry. "You were being self-righteous, too. Because if you want to see someone wolf down twice as much food in half as much time as my *schweschder*, you should look in the mirror, Conrad. Even more importantly, you should remember what the Bible says about people looking on outward appearances, but the Lord looking at the heart." He cleared his throat, then added, "And you aren't on your *rumspringa* anymore, Benuel. So if I hear another inappropriate comment about *weibsmensch* from you, no matter who it is, I will hold you accountable before the elders and deacon. Understand?"

There was a silence and then one or both of them mumbled something Susannah couldn't catch. Sensing the interaction was over, she sprinted toward the house as quickly as she could so when Peter came out, he wouldn't know she'd overheard everything.

She almost didn't make it to the kitchen before dropping into a chair, dizzy with emotion. Susannah felt hurt and humiliated by what Conrad had said about her and Eva. She also felt angry. *Really* angry. So angry, she could hardly see straight. Or maybe it was tears that blurred her vision. Closing her eyes, she buried her face in her dirty hands and wept.

Oddly, it wasn't just Conrad's words and the other men's reactions that caused her to cry; it was also Peter's response to them. As grateful as Susannah was that he'd confronted their attitudes, Peter's reaction left her feeling frustrated and confused. *I've never heard him speak so fiercely,* she thought. *If he really believes that it's ungodly and unkind to judge each other by our outward appearances, then he was being hypocritical to end our courtship because I'm overweight.* Either that, or she was wrong and their breakup had absolutely nothing to do with how heavy she'd gotten. In which case, she was determined to do whatever she could to find out his *real* reason for calling off their courtship.

For now, she was going to take a long, hot shower. *The men will have to finish picking potatoes without me,* she decided. *And if Conrad or Jacob wants dessert with supper, they'll have to bake it themselves, because I'm going to hide the funny cake on them.* But first, she was going to cut herself a nice, big piece.

Chapter Nine

Susannah had been overjoyed to hear that the specialist told Lydia her wrist was healing better than he'd expected and he didn't think surgery would be necessary. The news seemed to increase Lydia's confidence in her ability to stay on her own and to be more active. Still, Susannah was relieved when it rained on Saturday, because that meant Marshall and the boys would be home while she went to Eva and Peter's house.

However, to her surprise, Lydia announced at breakfast that she'd decided to spend the afternoon canning applesauce with Almeda and a couple other women in the district. "I'll probably be more of a nuisance than a help, but I'll enjoy chatting with the other *weibsleit* again." She asked Susannah, "What time will you be done at Eva's *haus*? Marshall or the *buwe* can swing by to get me after they pick you up."

Before Susannah could answer, Marshall asked, "Eva Lambright's *haus*?"

"*Jah.* Didn't I tell you? I'm going to visit her and Dorothy. And to show Eva how to make a few recipes."

"That's her *mamm*'s responsibility, not yours."

Susannah was startled by her grandfather's comment. Was he worried that Dorothy might feel like Susannah was taking her place by teaching her daughter how to cook? "*Jah*, but I don't think her *mamm* will mind. I've heard that Dorothy's been ill lately, so I think both she and Eva will be grateful to have a little help."

"What about your obligation to help Lydia? She's got a broken wrist. There's nothing wrong with Dorothy Lambright."

Susannah was so surprised she was speechless. She'd always known her grandfather was rough around the edges, but he almost sounded ruthless. How did he know whether Dorothy was genuinely ill or not?

"I'm going to be gone for most of the afternoon, so I won't need help, Marshall, but if I do, you and the *buwe* will be here," Lydia reminded him in a quiet but firm voice. "Susannah always considers her obligations to our *familye*. She already told me she'd prepare lunch for us before she leaves this morning. She'll be home in time to prepare supper, too."

Susannah added, "I don't mind walking if you're concerned about the *gaul* making too many trips in the rain, *Groossdaadi.*"

"That's not my concern." Marshall stood up and put on his hat. "Jacob can take you and Conrad will pick you up. There's no need for you to walk or for the Lambright *buwe* to give you a ride home."

After he strode out to the barn, Susannah pondered why he seemed so stern. It was almost as if he had a grudge against Dorothy Lambright. *Maybe he thinks she didn't do a gut job raising Hannes, because he went through a rebellious phase during his* rumspringa. But that didn't make sense, because Benuel's wild running-around period had lasted a lot longer than Hannes's had, and Marshall had a lot of respect for the extended Heiser family.

Oh, well. It was frustrating enough that Susannah didn't know for certain why Peter had broken up with her; she didn't want to waste her time playing a guessing game about what Marshall was thinking, too. Collecting the dirty breakfast dishes, she concluded, *Whatever* Groossdaadi*'s concern about Dorothy is, it doesn't have anything to do with me and I'm not going to let it interfere with my relationship with her.*

"How is Susannah going to help you cook if you've got dishes piled up in the sink and on the counters?" Peter was unable to keep the annoyance out of his voice. The house was a mess—at least, compared to how orderly Susannah and Lydia kept their home. He should have tried to help Eva straighten it up earlier, but he'd half expected Marshall would have found a reason to prevent Susannah from coming. "You've also got *schul* papers spread around the living room."

"We won't be cooking in the living room," Eva retorted. "Don't worry, I'll clean everything up. Besides, this is my territory, not yours. I don't *kumme* into the workshop and tell you and Hannes how to organize your supplies."

"I wish you would," Hannes quipped. "We've got a big delivery of cedar coming today and we still can't figure out how we're going to fit all of it on our storage racks."

Peter ignored their kidding around. He lifted a dirty coffee mug from the counter and set it with the others in the sink. Then he rinsed a dishcloth so he could wipe up the brown ring the cup had left behind. "Is *Mamm* up yet?"

"Not unless she's hiding under the table," Eva joked, making Hannes laugh. "What are you so nervous about? Susannah is coming to see me and *Mamm*, not to inspect the *haus*."

"It's Susannah!" Hannes exclaimed and Peter's stomach dropped as he glanced toward the door, thinking his brother meant she'd arrived early. But then Hannes asked Eva, "*She's* the *weibsmensch* Peter wants to court, isn't she?"

"She is *not*," Peter objected, surprised by how menacing his own voice sounded.

"*Jah*, she is. Isn't she, Eva?" Hannes persisted.

Peter threw the dishcloth into the sink. "You two don't know what you're talking about and it's a sin to spread false rumors," he protested, glaring at his brother and sister. He knew how sanctimonious he sounded, given that they'd only been teasing him, but he couldn't risk that what they were saying in jest might somehow get back to Marshall.

Hannes rolled his eyes but Eva turned serious. "I may be a *bobbelmoul* sometimes, but I haven't spread any rumors, Peter. Dorcas's little *schweschder* is the one who told me you probably liked Dorcas. She said you gave her a ride home alone from Marshall's *bauerei* a while ago." Eva blinked her big eyes repeatedly, as if she was on the verge of tears. "That's why I suggested we should give her a ride home from the frolic last *Samschdaag*, too. I was trying to be helpful. I thought if you were courting someone, it would cheer you up."

Peter was so astonished he couldn't speak: his sister had made the same assumption about him and Dorcas that Marshall had made. And, apparently, Dorcas's sister had made that assumption, too. The question was, did *Dorcas* think he wanted to court her? *Neh, she can't think that*...she *was the one who asked* me *for a ride. I never* offered *her one*, Peter mused as he tried to reassure himself.

To his sister, he said, "*Denki* for being concerned about me, Eva. And I do trust that you wouldn't deliberately spread rumors, especially not about our *familye*. But you're too young to be thinking about romance and who's courting who. And I don't need a matchmaker."

"You mean because you and Dorcas are *already* courting?" Her lips instantly sprang into a smile.

"Neh!" Peter objected vehemently. "And I have no intention of courting her, either."

Eva's shoulders drooped. "When she finds out, she's going to be really sad."

"I doubt it. I don't think she's any more interested in our *bruder* than he is in her," Hannes said knowingly, which came as a relief to Peter. He didn't want to court Dorcas, but neither did he want to mislead her or hurt her feelings.

"What makes you say that? Are *you* courting her?" Eva asked.

"Neh, but one of my friends is. I'd tell you who, but then Peter would accuse me of sinning by spreading rumors." Even without naming names, Hannes's answer was all the confirmation Peter needed to put his mind at ease.

"What are you three whispering about over there?" Dorothy asked from the doorway. To Peter's astonishment, she was completely dressed and she'd brushed her hair back into a neat bun and pinned on her prayer *kapp*. If it wasn't for her pale skin and the dark circles beneath her eyes, she would have looked like she had a year or two ago.

"Why are you up already, *Mamm*?" he asked.

"You know why—Susannah's coming to visit your *schweschder* and me. She should be here shortly so we've got to tidy the *haus*. You *buwe* ought to get to work, too."

So the two brothers put on their hats and coats and stepped out into the rain. As he walked toward the workshop, Peter felt ashamed for having felt ashamed. For worrying about what Susannah might think of his mother or the state of their house. It wasn't exactly that Peter thought she'd be judgmental. But he was still worried that she might unintentionally mention something about her visit in front of Marshall. And then the old farmer would have another reason to judge Peter's family as unfairly as he'd judged Peter.

Who cares what he thinks of us? He doesn't really *know me. And he certainly doesn't know* Mamm, *either.* Because if he did, he'd understand that it had taken her more effort to get up and get dressed at this early hour than it took for Marshall to harvest his entire farm. And thinking about it like that, Peter's insecurities melted away and his chest swelled from all the admiration he felt for his mother.

When Eva brought Susannah into the living room to say hello to her mother, she was startled by Dorothy's appearance. *How can* Groossdaadi *say she's not ill?* Susannah wondered as she plastered a smile on her face and returned Dorothy's warm greeting.

"Will you make us a cup of tea before you *meed* start

cooking?" she asked her daughter. When Eva left the room, she invited Susannah to sit down and then she said, "It's so *gut* to see you again. Tell me how you've been. And how is Lydia doing? Peter told me she broke her wrist."

Because Dorothy didn't start their conversation with comments or questions about her weight loss, Susannah immediately felt at ease in her presence and she shared openly. After telling her about her family back in Dover and her trip to Maine, as well as Lydia's good news about her arm, Susannah asked Dorothy how *she'd* been lately.

"As you can probably tell by looking at me, I've been a little out of sorts." Dorothy attempted to smile but her mouth slid into a frown and she teared up. "Ach, there I go again. I'm so moody. I pray about it, but..." Her voice trailed off.

Susannah was silent for a moment as Dorothy wiped her eyes. She didn't know whether Dorothy meant she was physically, emotionally or spiritually "out of sorts." But it wasn't really Susannah's business, so she didn't ask. Instead, she said softly, "I'm sorry you've been suffering... Is there anything I can do to help make things better?"

Dorothy audibly caught her breath in either a sob or a laugh. "You're one of the few people who has asked me what she could do to help me instead of telling me what I should do to help myself." A smile crept over her face as she said, "But the truth is, you've already done so much to help me."

"I have? How?"

"You've *kumme* here, to share some healthy recipes with my *dochder*. And you've prepared many hearty, *appenditlich* meals for my *suh* when I've been too tired to even pack him a lunch."

"It's my pleasure," Susannah replied. She told Dorothy that she'd learned about good nutrition when her father's health was failing and she listed the improvements he'd experienced since they'd changed their diets. "Not everyone is interested in changing what they eat, but I'm *hallich* that Peter appreciates what I make for lunch. And I hope Eva enjoys preparing the dishes I'm going to make with her today, too."

"I think she will. She works very hard to keep up with *schul* and take care of me and the *haus*. She cooks, too, but it's mostly frozen or canned food, so I think we'll all benefit from a change in our menu." Shivering, Dorothy adjusted her shawl around her shoulders. "You look as *wunderbaar* as ever but I notice you've lost weight since last summer. Is that a result of the healthy dietary changes you've made, too?"

"Jah." Dorothy's question was so matter-of-fact that Susannah didn't mind discussing her weight loss with her at all. "But I'm afraid some of my habits are slipping. I'd better get back on track soon, because I had so much more energy when I was eating well and getting enough exercise."

"Hmm. Maybe a change in diet is what I need, too," Dorothy mumbled thoughtfully.

Susannah nodded. "I was surprised how much it helped my *daed* and me. Although I was fortunate— the hospital connected us with a nutritionist first. She was a *wunderbaar* resource. I always thought we were eating healthy food, because we rarely bought anything from the store, but she taught me that even meals and desserts made from scratch can contain too much sugar or salt or carbohydrates."

Dorothy was a rapt listener and Susannah appreciated being able to share her excitement about what she'd learned without feeling she was being judged as boastful. "The nutritionist also emphasized that even though the *Englisch* lifestyle is much more sedentary than ours, it's still important for us to get aerobic activity for *gut* heart health. So my sister-in-law and I purchased a used stationary bicycle we put in the basement to use on rainy days when we can't take a walk outdoors."

"What a *schmaert* thing to do."

"That was also the nutritionist's idea. She thought it was worth a try although she told me most *Englischers* end up using their exercise equipment as clothes racks instead of for physical activity." Susannah giggled. "But I have to admit, sometimes Charity and I hang clothes on the handlebars of the bicycle, too."

As Dorothy threw her head back with laughter, Susannah was glad that her tearfulness had passed. Yet at the same time, her own mood momentarily flagged because seeing Dorothy again reminded Susannah how much she'd once anticipated being her daughter-in-law.

All morning as he restacked the shipment of cedar boards, Peter had been mulling over Hannes's suggestion that Susannah was the woman Peter wanted to court. His thoughts and feelings swung back and forth between hopeful wishing that he could become Susannah's suitor again to resentful acceptance of the fact that he couldn't.

So by the time he and Hannes walked up to the house for lunch, Peter's stomach was so jittery that he didn't know if he'd actually be able to eat anything. *That's* lappich. *I eat with Susannah every day. This is no different*, he reminded himself. *What's the worst that can happen—spilling my* millich *all over the table?*

No, the worst that could happen would be for Peter to say or do something that gave away the secret he could scarcely admit to himself: namely, that he was still in love with Susannah. He decided that the best way to try to prevent that from happening would be to say as little as possible. And given that his stomach was bouncing with anxiety, he decided he probably should *eat* as little as possible, too.

But when Hannes opened the door and a piquant aroma wafted through the air, he immediately felt hungry again. Then he heard his sister giggling at something Susannah said and Peter's shoulders relaxed, too. He grinned as he greeted them.

"Hi, Peter. Hi, Hannes," Susannah and Eva replied at the same time, which made them giggle again.

They act like two schweschdere, Peter thought. He immediately put the idea out of his head because it reminded him too much of Eva saying she wanted one of her brothers to get married so she could have a sister-in-law. He excused himself to go wash his hands and then Hannes took his turn. When Peter came back into the kitchen, Susannah was alone, peeking in the oven. She straightened up and turned to him.

"What are you looking at? The mess I've made?" she asked. "Usually I clean up as I go but we were having so much *schpass* I wasn't paying attention."

"I didn't even notice." Peter chuckled to think that he'd worried about a coffee-ring stain on the countertop. "Is my *mamm* reading in her room?"

"Actually, she's been taking a nap," Susannah replied nonchalantly, as if it was completely normal for an adult to take a nap before noon. "Eva went to ask if she wants to eat with us. If she's too tired, I'll keep something warm for her in the oven."

"Just make sure Hannes doesn't find it before she does," Peter warned her.

"Why? Does he eat as much as Conrad and Jacob?"

"He eats *more*."

"That's impossible."

"It's true," Peter insisted.

"I'll believe it when I see it," Susannah said in a saucy voice.

Peter didn't know how even the most casual conversation with her could make him feel so punchy, but if he didn't stop bantering with her like this, his butterflies would come back. And the food smelled too delectable for him to miss out on this meal.

Hannes returned to the room and a few minutes later, so did Eva and their mother. Dorothy looked much more tired than she'd appeared this morning. Or maybe it was just that her hair was mussed and her dress was wrinkled from lying down in it. They all sat down— Susannah was seated across from Peter—and he was about to say grace when he noticed his mother wasn't wearing her prayer *kapp*. He didn't want to embarrass her by drawing attention to her forgetfulness, but he knew she'd be upset if she realized she wasn't wearing it while they prayed.

Out of the corner of his eye, he noticed Susannah tug her own *kapp* strings, discreetly signaling Dorothy's oversight. It was such a small, simple gesture, but the amount of quiet dignity she extended to Peter's mother doubled his respect for Susannah.

"*Ach*, I forgot my *kapp*," Dorothy said, so Eva darted into her room to get it for her. When she had pinned it securely in her hair, Peter said grace. Then they passed around the platters of honey Dijon garlic chicken breasts, roasted vegetables and baked potato wedges that Susannah again referred to as French fries. Unlike during lunchtime at Marshall's house, this afternoon they ate slowly, simultaneously enjoying both the food and the pleasant conversation. Eventually, everyone but Hannes finished their meal. Peter caught Susannah's eye and gestured toward his brother with his chin, as if to say "See? I told you."

She glanced at the teenager. "I assume you liked the meal, Hannes?"

"*Jah.*" His mouth was too full for him to say anything else.

"Didn't I tell you what a *gut* cook Susannah is?" Peter asked proudly, not caring if anyone picked up on his obvious appreciation for her.

"*Denki*, Peter…but I didn't make this meal. Eva did." Hannes momentarily stopped eating. "Really?"

"Well, Susannah told me how to do everything," Eva quickly informed them.

"*Neh*, I just gave you the recipe. I couldn't have made this any better myself," Susannah said. "And, actually, if I had made it, the fries would have been burned to a crisp."

Peter chuckled and then the two of them recounted the story about the meal she'd ruined, how Benuel was going to eat the charred chicken, anyway, and what Peter had said to him about sanding it down. Everyone cracked up, especially Dorothy. *She may look tired, but she sure seems to be in a lively mood,* he noticed.

"Who wants dessert?" Eva asked.

"I do." Hannes popped the last potato wedge into his mouth.

Their mother's appetite was strong today and she said, "Me, too."

"Just a tiny sliver," Susannah told Eva.

"How about you, Peter?" his sister asked.

No, he didn't want dessert. Because that would mean their meal with Susannah was almost over. But since everyone was waiting for his answer he said, "*Jah,* please. Whatever it is, make mine a big piece."

After lunch, Dorothy offered to dry the dishes. Susannah could see how weak she was, but she didn't want to insult her by suggesting that she should go rest instead, so she gratefully accepted her help. However, as soon as they'd put away the last utensil, Dorothy admitted she needed to sit down in a comfortable chair in the living room. Close to tears, she said, "I *want* to help you *meed* cook, but I just feel drained."

"That must be frustrating," Susannah said, empathizing with the older woman. "But we did most of the prep work before lunch, so we don't have much left to do, anyway."

When Eva had stopped by the house with Hannes on Thursday, Susannah had given her some of the recipe cards she'd brought with her from Delaware so the young girl could purchase the ingredients they'd need ahead of time. Susannah had planned to help Eva make supper for their evening meal, which could be eaten again as leftovers on the Sabbath. She also wanted them to prepare a couple of dishes to refrigerate or freeze for later in the week.

As they worked together, it became clear to Susannah that, like most Amish girls her age, Eva was familiar with the basics of cooking. She just needed a few hints about the preparation and timing involved in making homemade meals, since she lacked experience cooking from scratch. The two of them had several pans sizzling on the stove when they discovered Eva had only bought half of the amount of ground turkey required for one of their recipes.

The Lambrights lived as far away from the main grocery store as Marshall and Lydia did, but there was a smaller, more expensive market nearby. Although it wasn't frequented by the Amish, Susannah suggested she could jog over there and pick up the turkey they needed.

"*Neh*, I'll go," Eva objected. "I'm the one who forgot to get it and it's raining."

From the other room, Dorothy called, "I'd go, but I'm too tired. Susannah, you should use our buggy and Eva can stay here and I'll help her keep an eye on the cooking. Take the black *gaul*. His name is Pepper."

Susannah agreed that was the best idea so she charged off to the barn. Pepper seemed a bit agitated and he had bits of bedding or dirt on his shoulders and flanks. Knowing that the harness could rub against the debris and give the animal a sore, Susannah decided to brush him off first. She spoke soothingly to him as she worked and he seemed more settled by the time she put on the harness.

As she was fastening the straps on the breast collar, Peter came into the barn, water dripping from the brim of his hat. He stopped short, as if surprised to see her. "Wh-where are you going? Is everything okay with *Mamm*?" he asked. There was a distinctly panicked tone to his voice and it occurred to Susannah that he must have been carrying an abiding concern about his mother's condition.

"Your *mamm* is fine." Having fastened the harness collar, Susannah paused to smile reassuringly at Peter. "We need something from the market over on Pine Street, so she told me I could take the buggy."

"Oh." He came closer and rubbed the horse's neck for a moment, then suggested, "Pepper can be a little skittish sometimes. The roads are slick and the *Englischers* drive pretty fast around here. Maybe I should go with you?"

Peter knew full well Susannah could handle the horse and buggy on her own. But he wasn't asking whether she needed help; he was asking whether she wanted his company. It reminded her of when he'd first asked if he could court her. The response she gave him now was the same as the one she'd given him then. "I'd like that. *Denki*." Then she added, "As long as it doesn't interfere with your work."

"*Neh*. Hannes ate three desserts. He has enough energy for both of us. I've just got to bring him that spare sawhorse over there and then I'll be right back."

Since the workshop was a good quarter of a mile away from the house and barn, Susannah had the horse and buggy hitched and was ready to go by the time Peter returned. After they got into the carriage and headed toward the small market, Susannah remarked, "It's been very pleasant spending time with your *mamm* and *schweschder* today. I'm sorry Dorothy hasn't been well, though."

"Denki."

Susannah didn't know whether his answer was so succinct because he was concentrating on the road ahead or because he didn't want to talk about his mother's condition. She'd gathered that their family was guarded about his mother's health and Susannah wasn't going to pry. But she did want him to know she cared, so she said, "I worried a lot when my *daed* was ill. But it helped me to know a lot of people were praying for him. I'll be praying privately about your *mamm*, too."

"I appreciate that, Susannah." Peter glanced over at her, his eyes more gray than blue in this light. His voice was husky when he added, "I—I'm sorry I wasn't a source of support for you when your *daed* was hospitalized. That must have been a very difficult time."

"Jah, it was," she admitted. *It was a difficult time because of my* daed*'s health and it was a difficult time because you'd broken up with me.* Sensing this might be a good opportunity to find out why Peter had called off their courtship, Susannah considered bringing up the subject. Asking him about it outright.

But she was torn. What if she found out her weight gain really *was* the reason? Or what if he still adamantly refused to say why he'd broken up with her one way or the other? It would put a damper on the delightful time she'd spent with him and his family. So as they slowed down, nearing an intersection, she just added, "But *Gott* is *gut* and His grace was—and is—sufficient for us."

"Jah," Peter solemnly agreed. They halted at the stop sign, opposite an *Englisch* vehicle, and waited for their turn to pull forward. As they started up, they passed another buggy headed in the opposite direction. Peter

craned his head in a backward glance. "Was that your *groossdaadi*?"

His voice sounded almost as alarmed as it had sounded when he'd asked her if his mother was okay. It occurred to Susannah that Peter might be worried that whoever was in the other buggy had seen them together and assumed they were courting. And it was fully possible that Marshall had been traveling down this street on his way back from dropping off Lydia at Almeda's *haus*. However, Susannah tried to reassure Peter, and said, "I didn't notice who it was. But if my *groossdaadi* mentions he saw us out today, I'll just explain the situation and he won't give it a second thought."

From the grim expression on Peter's profile, Susannah could tell he was unconvinced. *What's he so worried about?* she wondered as they pulled into the grocery-store parking lot. *We're not courting, so we don't have anything to hide. And even if we were courting and* Groossdaadi *saw us out together, what's the worst that could happen? It's not as if he'd try to prevent us from seeing each other.*

Chapter Ten

"The turkey meatballs we made for last night's supper turned out *appenditlich*," Eva told Susannah after church on Sunday as they were heading toward the staircase to go and help the other women prepare and serve lunch. "There was only one slight problem."

"What was that?" Susannah asked.

"Hannes and Peter liked them so much they didn't leave any for leftovers for today's supper!"

"*Ach.* I should have warned you. My *familye* enjoys those meatballs so much that I always set some aside ahead of time so there will be enough for a second meal," Susannah replied, chuckling. "Did your *mamm* go downstairs already?"

Susannah wanted to say hello to Dorothy, and to Peter. She also wanted to let him know that Marshall hadn't mentioned anything about seeing them on the road yesterday. Peter had been so uptight on the way home from the market, he'd hardly spoken two words to her, so she'd hoped to find a way to chat with him in private and put his concern to rest.

"*Neh.* She was tired so Peter brought her home as

soon as the sermon ended. But Hannes came in a separate buggy, so I get to stay for lunch for once."

"I'm *hallich* you get to stay, but I hope your *mamm* is okay."

Smiling, Eva assured her, "She'll be fine once she has a nap. And she told us last night that after speaking with you, she decided she's going to go see a nutritionist. She thinks her problem might be related to her diet—not that she's depressed." Eva clapped her hand over her mouth. Her voice was muffled as she said, "I wasn't supposed to tell anyone that."

"It's okay. I promise not to mention a word about it to anyone." Susannah was aware that some—but not all—Amish people she knew believed depression was akin to laziness, or that it was an indication that someone wasn't praying enough or was too self-focused. She even suspected that's why Marshall had claimed that Dorothy wasn't actually ill. Attitudes like that were probably why the Lambright family had been so secretive about Dorothy's condition, too. Susannah touched her young friend's arm. "It's *gut* that your *mamm* is going to consult a nutritionist, but no matter what her condition is, the important thing is that she receives help and starts to feel better. I'll be praying about that."

"Denki."

"For today, let's make sure the *weibsleit* send some of the lunch leftovers home with you. Just don't let your *brieder* see the food until suppertime," Susannah suggested, restoring the smile to Eva's face.

"Jah. Especially since I heard that some of the *weibsleit* made apple-butter pie for dessert today!"

A few minutes later, as Susannah was carrying a tray of bread, church peanut butter, cheese and homemade bologna from the basement to the gathering room, she passed Dorcas in the stairwell. To her dismay, her friend uttered a greeting, but barely glanced her way. However, when lunch was over and the last serving trays and dishes had been washed and put away, Susannah felt a tap on her shoulder.

"Can I speak to you?" Dorcas asked, still not meeting Susannah's eyes. "I thought we could walk to my *haus* together and I can give you a ride home."

Susannah was tickled that Dorcas wanted to spend the afternoon with her. "*Jah.* Of course. I just need to go tell *Groossdaadi* and Lydia they can leave without me." She raced outside and let them know, then circled back to where Dorcas was waiting for her beneath a large maple tree that was just starting to change from green to crimson.

Susannah thought she was seeing the reflection of its color on Dorcas's cheeks, but as her friend began speaking, she realized she was red-faced from embarrassment. "Oh, Susannah, I'm so sorry," she blurted out, as soon as they began walking. "My behavior toward you the past couple of times we've seen each other has been hurtful and unkind and I hope you'll forgive me."

"Of course I'll forgive you," Susannah told her. "And I'd like you to forgive me, too…except I'm not quite sure what I've done to offend you."

"You haven't really done anything. Nothing worth my getting so upset about, anyway."

"Even so, I'd like to know what's been troubling you."

"Well, I guess I was… I was annoyed because the day I came to the *bauerei*, I'd been on my feet at work all morning and then I walked all the way to your *groossdaadi*'s *haus*. Even though I was tired, I was so *hallich* to see you that I didn't mind taking another walk because you'd said you'd been cooped up in the *haus* for days. But then when it started to rain, it seemed as if you didn't even care if I got wet. All you cared about was getting exercise."

Now Susannah felt *her* cheeks turning as crimson as the maple tree's leaves. "*Ach.* That was so selfish of me. No wonder you were upset. I'm very sorry, Dorcas."

"It's okay. I should have said something at the time instead of holding it against you. I think I was also a little upset because, well, because when we first saw each other I was so *hallich* for you about your weight loss. But you didn't even notice that I've lost weight, too." She touched her stomach. "I still have a long way to go, but I'm trying really hard. I understand that you don't like anyone to talk about your weight loss, but I need encouragement."

She pulled her friend to a stop and looked into her eyes. "I'd be *hallich* to encourage you however I can, Dorcas. But to be honest, that day you came to the *bauerei*, the only thing I noticed was how *wunderbaar* it felt to finally see my friend's pretty face in person again after exchanging so many letters."

"That's really sweet, but you don't have to say that just because I've been feeling insecure about my outward appearance. Deep down, I know what we look like to each other isn't nearly as important as what our hearts look like to *Gott*."

"I know you know that. But I'm not complimenting you for any reason other than I'm telling you the truth about how I see you," Susannah asserted adamantly, peering into her eyes.

"Denki." Dorcas nodded, accepting the compliment. As the two women continued walking, she remarked, "I shouldn't have given you such a hard time about riding in the buggy with Benuel. I know you're not interested in him."

"It's all right. I've had to readjust to some of the customs and beliefs here in New Hope. In my district, it doesn't necessarily mean a *weibsmensch* is interested in being courted by a *mann* just because she accepts a ride with him." Susannah took a deep breath before asking the question she wasn't sure she wanted her friend to answer. "Speaking of accepting a ride with a *mann*… Are you interested in having Peter for your suitor?"

When Dorcas went silent and Susannah noticed she was blushing, she felt like weeping—a response that showed Susannah just how much she'd been wishing *she* could have Peter for *her* suitor again. She held her breath until Dorcas replied, *"Neh.* I'm not. I just rode with him out of envy. It was as if I was trying to prove that you may have lost weight, but I had a more attractive personality." She covered her face with her arm. "It was so childish of me…and I'm really sorry."

Susannah burst out laughing. "It's fine. And you *do* have a more attractive personality than I've had lately. Which is one of the many reasons I know you'll have a suitor like you've been hoping for very soon."

"Um. Maybe sooner than you think." Dorcas shyly dipped her head. "Samuel Wittmer, Isaiah's *bruder*, is courting me."

"Dorcas!" Susannah yelped toward the sunny sky. "That's *wunderbaar*! Why didn't you tell me?"

"Because he just asked me on *Dinnschdaag*. He said he wanted to ask me sooner but he heard a rumor that

Peter was my suitor. Which serves me right for asking for rides from him, I guess." Both women chuckled and then Dorcas remarked, "The idea of Peter courting me is unimaginable."

Susannah stuck her fists on her hips. "Now why would you say a thing like that?"

"Because of the way I saw him looking at *you*. I think he's enamored with you, Susannah."

Her heart pitter-pattered; Dorcas was saying the same thing Lydia had claimed. Both of them couldn't be wrong, could they? "I'm not so sure about that," Susannah replied. She wasn't so *unsure* about it, either. The only thing she did know for certain was that the idea of having Peter as her suitor again had become a lot more appealing ever since she'd heard him admonishing Conrad and Benuel for their comments about her weight. Yet, she still had her doubts, which she voiced to Dorcas. "Maybe he just likes me again because I've lost weight."

"*Neh*. The way he looked at you at the frolic the other day was the same way I used to notice him look at you the summer you were courting."

"*Jah*, but during the summer he was courting me I wasn't as heavy as during the winter he broke up with me," Susannah pointed out.

Dorcas shrugged. "I guess I can see why someone might draw that conclusion. But I've known Peter a long time and I've never fully believed that your weight had anything to do with why he called off your courtship."

"Uh-oh. Are you saying the real reason was because of my *baremlich* personality?" Susannah teased.

"*Neh!* I'm just saying I don't think it was your weight."

"The problem is, *Peter* isn't saying what the reason

is." *And I'm not sure I can face his answer, anyway,* Susannah thought.

As they were chatting, a buggy slowed down and came to a halt on the shoulder of the road about twenty yards ahead of them. Benuel hopped out and exclaimed, "Hi, Susannah! You're just the *weibsmensch* I wanted to see."

"And *I'm* just the *weibsmensch* he apparently *can't* see," Dorcas muttered because he hadn't greeted her.

"Hi, Benuel," Susannah replied coolly as they neared each other. She didn't appreciate him ignoring Dorcas any more than Dorcas did.

"Can I talk to you privately?" he asked. "It's important."

"Now?"

"Dawn won't mind, will you?" he asked, grinning at Dorcas.

"*Neh.* I'll wait over there," she replied, graciously ignoring his error. She crossed the road and leaned against the split-rail fence bordering a meadow, which the women would cross as a shortcut on their way to Dorcas's house.

"This will only take *one minute*," Susannah called after her, emphasizing the words for Benuel's benefit. Then she turned to him. "What's so urgent it can't wait until tomorrow when we see each other on the *bauerei*?"

"Since you mentioned how much you like the trails at the gorge, I rounded up a group of people to go hiking together. I couldn't find you after *kurrich*, but Marshall told me you'd headed in this direction. We'll have to hurry to catch up with the others."

Susannah was incredulous that he'd assumed she'd

want to go hiking with him without even asking her first. Furthermore, it was rude of him to take her aside now, just so he wouldn't have to extend the invitation to Dorcas, too. "In case you didn't notice, I've already got plans for the afternoon—I'm taking a walk with my *gut* friend. I'm not about to just ditch her and take off with you."

He glanced across the road, to where Dorcas was leaning against the railing. "Okay, we can give Dawn a ride home first." He chuckled wryly. "Although it seems like she could use the exercise."

"Her name is *Dorcas* and she probably gets more exercise in a day than you do in three," Susannah replied hotly. "And my answer is still *neh*." She started to cross the street, but Benuel pulled on her hand and she spun back toward him.

"Wait," he urged her. Releasing her fingers, he whispered, "I didn't just search for you so I could ask you to go to the gorge. I wanted to ask to be your suitor."

Susannah had acquired a lot of experience turning down potential suitors in the last year, since she'd lost weight, so she knew a kind but firm response was the best way to decline. "*Denki* for the offer, Benuel. But my answer is *neh*."

His mouth dropped open in surprise and then he closed it again and his features turned hard. Narrowing his eyes, he shook his head at her, but he returned to his buggy and sped away without saying another word.

At least there's no doubt in his mind about whether I'm interested in him or not, Susannah thought. Which was more clarity than she had about Peter's feelings toward *her*.

* * *

On Sunday night, Peter was lying in bed, trying to focus on the blessings he'd received that weekend. Most notably, although his mother was as tired as ever—she'd fallen asleep during church again—her mood seemed to have improved. There was a spark of hope in her voice again, too. Peter attributed this to the conversation she'd had with Susannah about the health benefits she'd experienced after making changes to her family's diet. Dorothy was so excited about the possibility that some of these changes might benefit her, too, that she'd asked Hannes to use their business cell phone to schedule an appointment for her with a nutritionist. He and his siblings were encouraged that she was willing to seek medical help again.

The other blessing Peter was especially grateful for was that everything had gone smoothly with the lumber delivery. Sometimes they received the wrong amount of supplies, which caused a delay, but the shipment was exactly what they'd ordered. He and Hannes had organized the wood and other supplies in a way that it would be kept dry and allow them to work efficiently. So they were well-prepared to start crafting the tables beginning tomorrow.

Also, Eva was delighted to have tried out a few new recipes. Peter knew that Susannah's guidance had been a real confidence booster for his sister. It was a relief to know that if his mother's condition didn't improve soon and she still couldn't supervise Eva's cooking, the young girl had been emboldened to try new recipes on her own.

Yet in spite of these occurrences, Peter wrestled with worry and resentment. He was still deeply concerned about his mother's health, of course. *What if she goes to a nutritionist and finds out that changing her diet doesn't improve her health? Will that make her even more resistant to consulting a different type of* dokder *in the future?* he wondered.

He also fretted about whether or not he and Hannes would meet the deadline for the wedding project. Although Peter preferred to simply agree to a project and then keep his word, many *Englischers* insisted on writing up contracts. This particular couple stipulated that if Peter and Hannes didn't deliver the full number of tables on time, they'd face a steep financial penalty. Peter intended to work every evening with his brother, but what if one of them became ill? Even one missed day of work could jeopardize the entire outcome of their endeavor.

But what Peter struggled with more than anything else was his resentment about Marshall's disparaging attitude toward him. Even if he'd only meant it as a token gesture, Peter found it insulting that when Marshall had gone to the doctor with Lydia on Thursday afternoon, he'd asked Benuel to keep an eye on the farm and crew. It wasn't that Peter wanted to be put in charge himself. It was that the very notion of someone "keeping an eye on" him and the rest of the crew was demeaning.

While Jacob and Conrad may have needed occasional supervision or instruction, overall, they were diligent and skilled young men. And as a matter of fact, Peter had far more harvesting experience than Benuel and he was far more industrious, too. *If anyone needs someone keeping an eye on him and monitoring his behavior, it's* Benuel, Peter ranted to himself. *Not just because of all the breaks he takes when he should be working, but because of the way he speaks about* weibsleit. *Especially about Susannah.*

Granted, Peter had effectively put an end to those kinds of comments when he'd confronted Conrad and Benuel in the barn after hearing them joking about Eva's and Susannah's weight. And both of the young men had mumbled apologies. So Peter knew it would be unforgiving to continue to hold their behavior against them. But what bothered him was that Marshall didn't seem to understand that Benuel was the kind of young man who still needed to be told to watch his mouth in the first place.

I don't want Marshall to think more highly of me than he does of Benuel just because Benuel is immature or because he's used inappropriate language, Peter told himself. *But I resent it that Marshall regards me as a lesser* mann *because he thinks I'm not a* gut *steward of the money* Gott *has given me. Especially since that's not even true!*

But it didn't matter what Peter wanted. The fact was, Marshall favored Benuel, probably because it was well-known in the district that Benuel had prospered financially when he'd lived among the *Englisch* and apparently he'd saved most of his income. *I'm sure Marshall would* wilkom Benuel into his familye *if he started courting Susannah and their courtship leads to marriage.* The thought made Peter's heart clench like a fist within his chest.

He would have liked to think the notion of Benuel marrying Susannah was a preposterous idea. However, at church this morning, as he'd been unhitching Pepper from the buggy, he'd overheard Benuel inviting Isaiah Wittmer to meet him and Susannah at the gorge to go hiking. "Bring Hannah," he'd said, referring to the woman Isaiah was going to marry soon. "We'll have a lot of *schpass* together—just the four of us."

"You're courting Susannah?" Isaiah had asked.

"Not yet, but I hope to ask her very soon. Who knows? Maybe by this time next year I'll be looking forward to my *hochzich,* just like you're looking forward to yours right now."

Their exchange had bothered Peter so much that he'd actually felt nauseated. So when his mother had said she wasn't sure she'd have enough energy to stay for lunch after church, Peter quickly volunteered to take her home. But his stomach never did settle down; he hadn't even been able to eat any of the leftovers Eva had brought home from church for their supper.

I doubt very much Susannah would accept Benuel as her suitor, he thought, but it was only a small consolation. Because whether or not Benuel courted Susannah, it didn't change the fact that there was absolutely no possibility that *Peter* could ever be her suitor again. It was so infuriating. So unjust. And it grieved him so deeply he almost wished Susannah hadn't returned to New Hope, so he wouldn't have to remember all he'd given up.

But the hard truth was, he'd made an agreement with Marshall and now he had to abide by his promise to not court his granddaughter. Peter rolled over on his side and was almost asleep when he was struck by a new realization: *I may have agreed never to court or socialize with Susannah, but I never promised I wouldn't talk with her, laugh with her and enjoy her company for as long as she's on the* bauerei.

He'd already been doing that to some extent, but he

intended to do it more frequently and more fully. He was tired of hanging his head. Of flinching every time Marshall looked at him askance. Of acting like a teenager who was worried he'd get caught courting a girl in his father's buggy. *What's Marshall going to do about it? He can't tell Susannah about our arrangement—he'd be breaking his word. And he can't ban me from the* bauerei *because he needs my help too much.*

Suddenly, his stomach felt calmer than it had felt all day and he could hardly wait to eat lunch tomorrow.

Susannah sensed a certain frostiness in Benuel's attitude toward her during lunch on Monday afternoon. But having been rejected herself, she'd understood why it may have been uncomfortable for him to have to sit next to her at the table and make small talk after she'd just turned down his offer of courtship the day before. So she tried to ease the tension with lighthearted chatter.

"Eva told me you and Hannes enjoyed the meatballs we made on *Samschdaag*," she commented to Peter.

"*Jah.* I enjoy everything you make."

"*Denki.*" Susannah could feel her cheeks flush as Lydia raised an eyebrow at her. She was so flustered that she kept prattling away. "She said you *menner* devoured all of them and she didn't have any leftovers for your *Sabbaat* supper. That used to happen at my *haus*, too. I'd tell my little nieces and nephews how many they were allowed to eat and we'd count them out together as I put them in the serving dish. But then my *bruder* would take twice as many as he was supposed to and the *kinner* would get upset because he'd eaten some of their share, too."

Susannah stopped to take a sip of milk before continuing. "One morning, my youngest nephew must have heard me telling Charity that I was making meatballs for supper, because he brought home his number line from *schul* and set it near his *daed*'s place at the table. He wasn't being naughty—he thought he was being helpful. We laughed so hard we cried. Now when I make meatballs, I just set aside whatever I need for leftovers for the next day before I serve them. And my *bruder* is not allowed to have more than he can count on one hand." Everyone except Benuel and Marshall had a good laugh over Susannah's story.

"You should get a number line for Conrad," Jacob suggested. "That's his third helping of applesauce."

"Isn't it *wunderbaar*? Lydia made it at a frolic this weekend."

"I hardly helped make it—Almeda and Lovina did. I couldn't peel any apples with my broken wing here." She held up her arm. "But I did help whisk ingredients for the apple-butter pies they brought to *kurrich* yesterday."

"It was *appenditlich*," Peter said, complimenting her. "Eva brought home leftovers and I had a piece for breakfast this morning."

"Oh, that's right—I forgot apple-butter was your favorite autumn pie," Susannah said without thinking until she noticed Lydia shoot her an odd look. In an attempt to cover her slipup, she brightly announced, "My favorite pie is peanut-butter pie. Especially the way my *mamm* used to make it—Lydia's the only person who makes it exactly the same way. Last summer she used to make one at least once a week when I was visiting. Between my *groossdaadi* and me, we'd polish it off within two days, wouldn't we, *Groossdaadi*?"

Marshall barely grunted in acknowledgment of Susannah's question. At exactly the same time, Benuel remarked, "That must have been when you were still overweight."

Both responses stung, but at least Susannah understood why Benuel was making a wisecrack; she had no idea why her grandfather was being so prickly.

"That remark was inappropriate, Benuel," Peter stated in a low, controlled voice.

"What?" Benuel acted surprised, turning his palms upward. "I just meant that I can't imagine Susannah eating that much food anymore."

Marshall abruptly rose to his feet. "Time for work," he said and pointed toward the door. All of the young men scrambled outside, except for Peter, who finished the last three spoons of his applesauce first.

"*Denki*, Lydia and Susannah." He put on his hat and walked past Marshall.

As soon as Peter closed the door behind him, Marshall sat back down at the table. Susannah didn't understand what was going on, but it didn't take long for her to find out. "Has he asked to be your suitor?" her grandfather asked bluntly.

Most Amish parents or grandparents she knew didn't directly ask their children and grandchildren about their courtships. But Susannah figured her grandfather hadn't appreciated Benuel's comment and he was concerned about her having a suitor who was rude to her. So she openly admitted, "*Jah.* But don't worry, I turned him down. I think that's why he made the remark he made at lunch, but it's okay, *Groossdaadi*—I know how to handle it."

Her grandfather rattled his head, as if he hadn't heard

right. "You mean *Benuel* asked to court you and you said *neh*?"

"*Jah*. That's right."

"Has Peter asked to court you, too?"

The answer just spilled from her lips. *"Neh."*

"*Gut*. Because I'd prefer you didn't socialize with him."

It was Susannah's turn to wiggle her head. "Why not?"

"I have my reasons," Marshall answered tersely and stood up as if the subject was closed.

Drawing her spine upward so she was sitting as straight as she could, Susannah stopped him when she said, "I respect your opinion, *Groossdaadi*, but I'm twenty-three years old and I'll make my own decisions about courting. If you'd like to share the reason you wouldn't want me to accept Peter for a suitor, I'll give it my full consideration. But otherwise, I can't abide by your wishes in the event that Peter asks to court me." Her legs felt shaky even though she was seated.

Marshall opened his mouth and then closed it again. Then he left. Susannah leaped to her feet and started clearing the table in a whirlwind of activity. "He is being *so* unreasonable," she complained, more to herself, under her breath. "And *so* controlling."

Lydia, who had been uncharacteristically silent during their discussion, spoke up now. "I know you're angry with your *groossdaadi* and you probably have *gut* reason to be. But his intention isn't to be controlling—it's to take care of you. He thinks he's asking you to do something that's for your own *gut*."

"I don't need him to take care of me. I'm twenty-three years old!" Susannah said for a second time, waving a dirty serving spoon in the air. "*I* can decide what's *gut* for me and what's not. And *I* can decide who I want for a suitor."

"I agree," Lydia said calmly. "And I'm not saying you shouldn't make your own decisions about who to court. But you should keep in mind that your *groossdaadi* has made concessions for your opinion, too. It might help you not to feel so angry."

"What do you mean? What concessions has he made for *my* opinion?"

"Well, he's been eating the kind of foods that *you* think are *gut* for him, even though he's certainly old enough to decide for himself what he wants to eat, isn't he?"

"But—but that's not the same," Susannah stuttered.

"Why isn't it?"

Because I'm right! Susannah wanted to retort. But then she realized her grandfather might have wanted to say the same thing about Peter. She rinsed a plate under the faucet before coming up with a better answer. "Because *I'd* explain to him why it's not healthy to eat a lot of fat or too much sugar. He isn't explaining *anything* to me."

"I suppose you're right." Lydia sighed. "How about this… I'll try to find out what his reason is—or to convince him to tell you what it is. In the meantime, it would be nice if you'd refrain from batting your lashes at Peter in front of Marshall during lunch."

Susannah was going to protest that she didn't bat her lashes. But she knew what her stepgrandmother meant; how she felt about Peter came across in the way she looked at him, as well as in the way he looked at her. So instead, she said, "*Denki*, Lydia. I really appreciate your help."

Not that Peter's going to ask to court me, anyway. But maybe if I find out why Groossdaadi *doesn't want him to be my suitor, it will give me insight into why Peter broke up with me in the first place.*

Chapter Eleven

After lunch, when Marshall approached Peter and Benuel as they were loading barrels of potatoes into the buggy wagon, Peter half expected the farmer to tell him to go home—that he didn't want him to help with the harvest anymore and that he wasn't welcome on the farm. Worse, maybe Marshall would even say that he'd told Susannah about the arrangement they'd made and that she never wanted to see Peter again, either.

He recognized that his behavior toward her during lunch today had been inappropriate. He may not have behaved as brazenly as Benuel sometimes did, but in some ways, Peter had acted as if he was Susannah's suitor. He'd complimented her, laughed at everything she'd said and come to her defense when Benuel made an inappropriate remark. None of Peter's actions was necessarily wrong, but his attitude while he was doing them had been one of defiance. It was as if he was saying to Marshall, "You can't tell me what to do." He'd even refused to immediately leave the house when Marshall ordered everyone to get back to work. But instead of making him feel more manly or powerful, Peter's actions had made him feel juvenile and rebellious. And he knew that in this instance he deserved whatever rebuke Marshall had in store for him.

Benuel must have been even more nervous than he was because Peter noticed his hands were shaking as Marshall approached. When the farmer cleared his throat, both of the young men immediately turned from their barrels to give him their full attention.

"My wife has invited you to share our lunch because she wants you to have *gut* hot meals in your stomachs when you're harvesting. But if your words or actions demonstrate disrespect for anyone—including each other—you won't be *wilkom* at the table again. Understand?"

"*Jah.* I'm sorry, Marshall," Peter apologized. But Marshall wasn't looking at him; he was staring at Benuel.

"*Jah.* Sorry." After Marshall walked away, Benuel blew all the air out of his cheeks, sounding every bit as relieved as Peter felt. Then they both resumed their work, eager to put the incident behind them.

When lunchtime rolled around on Tuesday, Peter made a point of *not* speaking to Susannah, who didn't say much to him, either. Which didn't mean he wasn't acutely aware of her presence; especially when she shifted in her chair and their knees bumped against each other's beneath the table.

But he didn't act on his impulse to tell her he'd never tasted roasted garlic potatoes before, but they were so good he hoped she planned to share the recipe with his sister so she could make them, too. And he didn't sneak a chance to confide that his mother had made an appointment with a nutritionist the following week, thanks to Susannah's encouragement. Nor did he say half a dozen other things he would have liked to tell her, such as that the dark green dress she was wearing made her eyes look more golden-brown than ever.

By Wednesday, the quietness at the table felt a little more normal again; instead of being a strained or awkward situation, they had the kind of silent meal that happened because everyone was enjoying their food too much to speak. Although, in Peter's case, he was so tired from working late at the workshop the evening before, he could hardly hold up his head, much less hold a conversation. It was probably the only time he would have preferred to spend his lunch break alone outside, or in the barn, where he could have slept instead of eaten. However, once he finished his second helping of ham and scalloped potatoes—something Susannah said she'd made especially for Marshall, since it was one of his favorite dishes—he felt invigorated again.

Two hours later, the buggy wagon was full of barrels and Peter headed out to the potato house. When he returned, he was surprised to see Susannah crossing the lane in the direction of the fields. She and Lydia had been taking walks around the property in the afternoons lately, but today she was alone. When she saw him approaching, she changed her direction and hurried toward him. Noticing the distraught expression on her face, Peter brought the horse to a halt and jumped down from the buggy wagon.

"Susannah, what's wrong?"

"It's my *groossdaadi*. He threw his back out and he's in agony," she said breathlessly.

"That's *baremlich*." Peter shielded his eyes to scan

the fields. "Where is he? Does he need help getting to the *haus*?"

"*Neh*. He's already there. The *buwe* helped him—it took almost half an hour because he was in such pain. We've given him muscle relaxants and ice packs and helped make him as comfortable as we could with pillows. I was just going out to take Jacob's place picking so he can do the digging." Susannah looked tearful and Peter had to fight the urge to wrap his arm around her shoulders to comfort her. "It's the only thing I could think of doing to help. I gave Lydia a cowbell so she could ring it if she needed me to *kumme* in... I don't know. Do you think I'm making the right decision? Maybe I should stay at the *haus* with them."

Peter considered her question thoughtfully before answering. "Your *groossdaadi* is probably going to be unable to work the next week, so unless you help us pick, we won't finish harvesting before the first frost. I think that's what Marshall would prefer that you do. But maybe today you could take a break every hour or so to run back to the *haus* to check on your *groosseldre*? That might help you feel a little less anxious, right?"

"*Jah*. So would prayer. Will you pray for *Groossdaadi*? I'm too wound up to pray for him myself."

"Sure." So they bowed their heads and Peter asked the Lord to ease Marshall's discomfort and Susannah's anxiety, to give Lydia patience and to give all of them strength and endurance. When he opened his eyes again, he saw that Susannah's forehead was no longer wrinkled with lines, and although she wasn't smiling, she didn't look as if she was about to cry anymore.

As she'd done when she'd helped pick before, Susannah quickly worked her way up the rows. For some reason—perhaps he was still embarrassed about the remark he'd made to her on Monday—this time Benuel didn't seem interested in conversing with her, so he kept up a good pace, too. And even though Susannah ran back to the house every hour, her help enabled the crew to pick and transport roughly the same quantity of potatoes they would have if Marshall hadn't gotten injured.

"How much longer do you think it will take us to finish harvesting?" Jacob asked as they headed toward the barn to put away the equipment for the night.

"At this rate, we should be done by next *Mittwoch*," Peter replied. "At least, we'd better be—there's a frost forecasted for Thursday."

"My muscles are so sore. I can't wait to finish," Jacob said.

Peter's muscles were sore, too, but that didn't mean he wanted the harvest to end…because now he'd get to see Susannah *all* day, instead of only at lunchtime or in passing around the yard. And now Peter knew that when he spoke and joked and even flirted with her out in the fields, he wasn't doing it with a spirit of defiance toward her grandfather; he was doing it with a sense of deep affection for Susannah.

Susannah lay in bed for a good half an hour after waking on Sunday morning. She was really looking forward to observing the Sabbath at home. Her aching body needed the rest and she was eager to spend time reading the Bible and chatting with her grandparents. She felt as if she'd barely seen them the last four days, since she'd been so tired in the evenings that she usually collapsed into bed right after finishing the supper dishes.

Yet, as dirty and demanding as picking potatoes was, Susannah valued the opportunity to be outside almost the entire day, to exercise muscles she didn't ordinarily use and to contribute to the urgent goal of harvesting the rest of the crop before the first hard frost.

And, of course, she relished the chance to work alongside Peter. Whenever he wasn't transporting potatoes to the potato house or she wasn't running inside to make a meal or check on Lydia and Marshall, Susannah and Peter would harvest neighboring rows, matching each other's pace. On occasion, Jacob or Conrad would pick close by, too, when they weren't operating the digger. The boys were hard workers, but once in a while they'd pull a prank, like tossing a rotten, smelly potato at each other. But more often than not, Jacob and Conrad picked nearer to Benuel, who moved down the adjacent rows from the opposite end of the field, out of earshot of Peter and Susannah. She figured Benuel was avoiding being around her because he still felt slighted that she'd refused him as a suitor.

She was happy to give him his space, as his distancing allowed her the privacy to converse freely with Peter, which they often did. He'd tell her about how he and Hannes had completed their first wedding picnic tables, or he'd repeat something Eva had said happened at school. Peter also confided that his mother had made an appointment with a nutritionist the following week and he thanked Susannah for being so encouraging to her. Susannah, in turn, told Peter about what Charity had written in her most recent letter, or she'd give him an update on how Marshall had fared the previous evening. Regardless of whether they were chatting or silent, Susannah treasured the experience of working side by side with Peter; it was how she'd once pictured them tending their own garden, or fields, as a married couple.

And sometimes, she *still* pictured them that way. Or, at least, she'd let her imagination roam to the possibility that Peter might ask if he could be her long-distance suitor again. She had made up her mind that if he asked, she wouldn't answer him until he'd told her the reason he had previously decided they weren't a good match.

I wonder if Lydia has been able to find out what Groossdaadi*'s qualm is about Peter yet*, Susannah thought. But given how much pain Marshall was experiencing, Susannah doubted that Lydia would have added to his discomfort by bringing up an unpleasant subject. *Oh, well. It's not as if Peter has asked to be my suitor yet, so I don't need to consider Marshall's opinion right this minute.*

What she *did* need to do right this minute was get up and start breakfast, as the boys would be coming in from the barn shortly. But her mind was more limber than her body and it took her twice as long to get dressed, brush her hair and make her bed as it usually did. When she went into the kitchen, Lydia was struggling to lift a heavy frying pan from the bottom cupboard.

"*Ach*, Lydia, you shouldn't be doing that. I've got it. You should go enjoy a cup of *kaffi* with *Groossdaadi*."

"We've already had one."

Susannah didn't realize she'd stayed in bed *that* late. "Where is he?"

"I sent him to the barn with the *buwe*." Lydia wiped her forehead with the back of her hand and then confided, "I love Marshall dearly and I'm sorry he's in pain. But let me just say I have a much better understanding of how *you* must have felt when you were stuck inside looking after me all day."

Susannah giggled. "It's *gut* that you've been taking him on short walks around the yard, though."

"*Jah.* That's what the chiropractor told us to do the last time he injured his back."

Peeking into the fridge, Susannah remarked, "It looks as if we're awfully low on groceries. I'm going to have to take a break from picking to go to the market."

"I suppose I could try to do the shopping myself," Lydia suggested.

"*Neh.* It would be too difficult for you to get in and out of the buggy or to load the groceries into the carriage. I'll go tomorrow. But for this morning all we have to eat is eggs and toast. And bacon. Lots of bacon."

"That will make Marshall *hallich.*"

"It will make me *hallich,* too. My appetite has doubled since I've been helping with the harvest." *And my waistline has been increasing, too,* Susannah thought. Lydia had been helping with food preparation as much as she was able to, but it had been challenging for Susannah to make healthy, fortifying meals, while also working in the fields. They'd been eating more potatoes and bread than she usually served, simply because they were convenient options in abundant supply. But all the starch had left Susannah feeling bloated and she looked forward to replenishing the pantry and fridge with other types of food.

Maybe today I can plan a healthier menu for the next three days until we're finished harvesting, she thought. While she'd hoped to make a special dessert on Wednesday to celebrate their accomplishment, she realized now that she had to give up on the idea. She hardly had time to put together a simple meal as it was.

After they'd eaten breakfast and worshipped together, Susannah served a customary light lunch— cheese and homemade bologna sandwiches. Because it was drizzling out and she was too tired to take a walk, she suggested that they all do a jigsaw puzzle together. But the boys were undeterred by the weather and went off on a hike, and Lydia wanted to sit at the kitchen table and write a letter to her sister. "I guess it's just you and me, *Groossdaadi*," Susannah said. She brought him an ice pack and rearranged his pillows, then set up the folding table right above his lap so he wouldn't have to stretch or shift in his chair.

After sitting down opposite him, she began rummaging through the box for the edge pieces. After their disagreement on Monday until the time he'd injured his back on Wednesday, Susannah had noticed she and her grandfather were politer than usual to each other. It felt unnatural, as if they were acquaintances instead of relatives. Then, following his injury, he'd been in too much pain to say much of anything to anyone. He didn't even join the crew for lunch, presumably because he didn't want to have to make or listen to small talk. Instead, Susannah would bring a tray to his room for him. But now that they were alone, she hoped to rebuild their usual rapport.

"This is like old times, when you lived in Dover and you and *mamm* and I used to do puzzles on the *Saabbat* together, remember?" she asked. When Marshall didn't answer, Susannah wasn't sure if he hadn't heard or if he was ignoring her question. Glancing up, she was surprised to see his eyes fixed on her.

"*Jah*, I remember," he replied and he sounded so nostalgic that Susannah thought she might cry. But then he added, "Your *mamm* used to get frustrated with us for looking at the box cover."

"That's because she thought it was cheating," Susannah recalled with a laugh.

She and Marshall worked on the puzzle in comfortable silence for another hour, until he said he needed to lie down flat for a while. Lydia also retreated to their room to nap, so Susannah perused the recipes Charity had sent. *Even though these are simple enough, I still don't know how I'll have the time to make them and help the* menner *pick potatoes*, she fretted, just as she heard a buggy coming up the lane.

Hoping it was Dorcas, Susannah darted outside to greet her. However, as she stepped onto the porch, she recognized it was Peter's buggy that had arrived. He had never come to the farm on a Sunday before now. Was it possible he was here to discuss a courtship with her? The prospect made her feel wobbly, so she held on to the railing for support.

But instead of veering toward the hitching post, Peter brought the horse to a halt near the side of the house, which meant he didn't plan on staying long. Disappointment washed over Susannah as she waited for him to come around to the porch. To her surprise, it was Eva who walked toward her carrying two large, foil-covered pans. Susannah rushed down the stairs to help her.

The young girl explained that Peter had mentioned Susannah was doing all the cooking and cleaning, as well as picking potatoes. So on Saturday, Eva had made two casseroles for Susannah to serve to the crew and her family.

"I used low-sodium broth instead of canned *supp* because that had too much sodium," she informed her. "Hannes tried it and said it was *gut*, but he'll eat anything so I hope everyone else likes it."

Susannah couldn't have been more grateful. "Why don't you and Peter *kumme* in for tea?"

"Peter didn't bring me. *Mamm* did."

"That's even better—I'd love to chat with her. So would Lydia. I'll go wake her."

"Neh!" Eva exclaimed. Then she lowered her voice. "I'm sorry but *Mamm's…* She's having a really bad day. That's why she didn't get out of the buggy. She didn't even want you to see her."

"I understand." Until now, Susannah hadn't really realized just how ashamed Dorothy was of her health condition. Or was it that she was fearful of being judged? "Please greet her for me and say *denki* for bringing you here to deliver these meals."

Later that evening, as she was lying in bed, it occurred to Susannah that maybe Dorothy's illness was the reason Peter had broken up with her. Maybe his mother didn't want anyone to find out she was depressed, as Susannah inevitably would have done if she'd ended up marrying Peter. *He's always been so loyal and devoted to his family—so that would explain why he couldn't give me a reason for breaking up with me.*

Certain she was right, Susannah whispered a prayer for the Lord to strengthen Dorothy. Then, out of the blue, she added, *And if it's Your will, please allow her to be my mother-in-law one day soon.* Because now that Susannah had finally figured out why Peter had broken up with her, there was nothing stopping the two of them from resuming their courtship.

On Monday morning, Peter traveled toward the farm feeling thoroughly energized. He'd spent the better part of the Sabbath either napping or praying for wisdom about his dilemma concerning the promise he'd made to Marshall. The more time Peter spent with Susannah, the more intense his desire to court her became. And he was confident that she would accept him as her suitor again if he asked. Yet he couldn't court her without breaking his word to Marshall, which was unacceptable to Peter. So his thoughts had kept circling around and around and ending up back at the same dead end.

However, as he was praying on Sunday it had occurred to him that there was *one* way he could court Susannah, and that was if Marshall released him from his promise. Until now, Peter couldn't have imagined the old farmer ever agreeing to do that. But because Marshall had injured his back and his crew had to take over the farm, Peter saw a perfect opportunity to show Marshall how responsible he was. To show him that he was a good steward—not just of his own money, but of a farm that didn't even belong to him. Maybe once the older man recognized that, he'd be more open to Peter courting Susannah.

The possibility was so exciting that as his buggy rolled down the lane on Marshall's property and Peter heard the birds' tuneful chirping, he couldn't resist whistling along with them. *It's already a* wunderbaar *day*, he thought. *And I haven't even seen Susannah yet.*

She always came out of the house a little later than Jacob and Conrad did in the morning, because she had to wash and dry the dishes and tidy the kitchen after breakfast. But he was surprised that Benuel hadn't arrived at the farm by the time the young men had hitched the digger to the horse and Peter had carried the barrels into the fields. When he commented about it to Jacob and Conrad, they shrugged.

"Last week he said he was going to take a long hike at the gorge yesterday, so maybe he got worn out and overslept," Jacob suggested.

Then Susannah came into the fields and Peter forgot all about Benuel's absence until she asked where he was. Peter said he expected him any minute, but a minute turned into an hour and then two more hours passed. Looking worried, Susannah suggested someone should ride out to the Heisers' house to find out what was keeping him.

"*Neh.* It's not worth the time we'd lose picking," Peter said, glancing toward the lane. "If he's not here by noon, I'll go over to the Heisers' *haus* during our break."

"You'd be willing to give up your lunch?" Susannah teased and hopped into his row to pick up a potato that she'd accidentally tossed over the barrel instead of into it. Standing inches in front of him, she playfully held up the spud. "I promise I'm not serving these again, if that's what you're worried about."

Knowing Conrad and Jacob had their backs turned and the view from the house was obscured by the barn, Peter closed his hand around hers and wrested the vegetable from her fingers. He tossed it into the barrel and said, "As I've told you before, I like *everything* you make. Even so, I'd sacrifice my lunch break if I had to for the sake of our crew." So she'd know he was completely serious, Peter peered into her eyes, then added, "But I'd really miss not sitting next to you at the table."

Beneath a residue of dusty dirt, a pink tinge rose in Susannah's cheeks. "I'd miss that, too. I *will* miss that," she replied and Peter understood. She didn't just mean she'd miss him if he left this afternoon: she meant she'd also miss him once the harvest was over. It was all the confirmation he needed to decide he *had* to talk to Marshall about releasing him from his promise.

His heart thundering as Susannah gazed up at him, Peter wanted nothing more than to lean forward and put his lips on hers. But since they weren't courting, that would literally be akin to stealing a kiss—and Peter was no thief. It was agony, but instead of stepping closer, he took a step back. And he was glad he did because a moment later, someone shouted, "Hey!"

He and Susannah both turned their heads to see Benuel heading toward them and the boys. One of his coat sleeves was flapping loosely as he walked and he appeared to be hiding something beneath his coat.

"Hi, Benuel. What have you got there—a kitten?" Susannah asked, instead of immediately asking why he was so late.

"Neh." Benuel pulled open one side of his coat to reveal his arm was in a sling.

"Voll schpass." Because Benuel was smirking, Peter had assumed he was pulling a prank. Or feigning a broken arm as an excuse for being late, which actually seemed in poor taste considering Marshall's and Lydia's recent injuries.

"I'm not kidding. I dislocated my shoulder pretty bad when I was helping my *onkel* move a generator before work this morning. The *dokder* popped my arm back into place but the dislocation tore a ligament," he reported. "Anyway, I can't use my arm for the next two days at least, and no heavy lifting for two weeks after that."

Jacob clutched the top of his hat in consternation and Conrad muttered, "That's *baremlich*." But it was difficult to tell if they were upset on Benuel's behalf or because they were losing a coworker.

"I'm sorry you got hurt." Susannah furrowed her forehead, obviously concerned about his well-being. "Are you in a lot of pain?"

"Well, it doesn't tickle."

Even though Benuel seemed dismissive of Susannah's empathy, Peter also expressed his concern, and then asked, "I don't suppose you can steer the horses and digger using only one hand, can you?"

"Lydia might have a better chance at doing that than I would," Benuel quipped. Then his expression turned somber. "My *onkel* is waiting for me in the van. We asked the driver to stop here on the way home from the ER. So I guess I'd better go tell Marshall I can't finish harvesting now."

He said goodbye to everyone, but before he walked away, Peter offered, "If your arm feels better next week and you're looking for a job, Hannes and I could use some help making picnic tables. We've got an urgent order."

"Really?" Benuel's eyes widened.

"Jah." Peter had seen his carpentry; Benuel did good work. And Peter intended to pay him for every table he completed instead of by the hour, so that would keep him on his toes. As far as Peter was concerned,

the arrangement might be the Lord's provision for both of them.

"Denki," Benuel said and started straggling through the fields toward the house.

"I should go with him and reassure *Groossdaadi* we can still finish the harvest by *Mittwoch* evening." Susannah bit her lip. "We can, can't we?"

"With *Gott*'s help, absolutely," Peter confirmed. *We'd better...because our future as a couple depends on it.*

Chapter Twelve

On Wednesday, as the sun was setting and Conrad and Jacob went into the house, Susannah lingered outside with Peter. After three days of arduous labor, they were grime-streaked and bone-weary, but also elated that they'd completed the harvesting.

"Are you sure you don't want to change your mind and *kumme* in for supper?" Susannah asked, even though he'd already hitched his horse and buggy. "There's plenty of food."

On Sunday afternoon, shortly after Eva and Dorothy had come by with the casseroles, Almeda and Iddo had dropped in for a visit. When Almeda had learned that Marshall wasn't able to work on the farm so Susannah was helping the crew, the deacon's wife offered to bring over a couple of meals. She also brought two more apple-butter pies, a batch of snickerdoodles and a container of pumpkin bars. On one hand, the extra food was terrific because it had meant Susannah didn't have to cook or go to the grocery store until tomorrow. However, it also meant she'd given in to the temptation to eat the treats more often than not. This morning she'd had to adjust the pins on her skirt again because it was too tight.

"*Denki*, but Eva is trying another new recipe and she'll be disappointed if I'm not home to taste it. Plus, I've got to help Hannes in the workshop as soon as we're done eating."

It was just light enough to see Peter's teeth as he turned toward her and smiled. Now that his horse and buggy were hitched, Susannah knew she should say goodbye and go inside and reheat her family's meal in the oven. But she figured Lydia was capable of doing that, and besides, this was probably the last time she'd see Peter until they went to church on Sunday.

"I'm sure if *Groossdaadi* was feeling better, he'd *kumme* out and thank you for all your help." At least, that's what she hoped he'd do. A breeze lifted her *kapp* strings and Susannah shivered, drawing her sweater closer around her torso.

"You're cold. I should leave," Peter suggested. But he didn't move away from her; he moved closer. Leaning down, he whispered into her ear, "If we were courting, I could give you a hug to keep you warm."

Susannah caught her breath. "If that's a question, the answer is *jah*."

"*Jah*, I can court you or *jah*, I can give you a hug?"

She giggled. "Both."

"*Denki*, Susannah." Peter wrapped his arms around her and held her close. "Is that better?"

"Much," she murmured into his chest.

As Peter journeyed home, he was aware that he'd put the cart before the horse by asking to court Susannah before speaking to her grandfather about their agreement. Yet despite acting in haste and against his better judgment, he didn't regret his behavior one bit. Holding Susannah in his arms for those few minutes had made Peter more motivated than ever to ask her grandfather to release him from his promise.

I'll talk to him before lunchtime tomorrow, he thought. Susannah had mentioned she was going to the grocery store late that morning, so he knew she wouldn't be at the house. He didn't know whether Lydia and the boys would be home, but he hoped if he told Marshall he needed to speak with him privately, the old man would oblige him and step outdoors.

That night he must have spent as much time praying about their upcoming discussion as he spent sleeping, and he yawned his way through the first few hours of the next morning. When it was finally time to leave, he informed Hannes, "I'm going to the farm. I'll be back in about an hour."

"The farm?" Hannes sounded surprised.

"*Jah.* And no complaints about working alone," Peter warned, scowling at him.

"I'm not complaining—especially not after all you've done for me, *bruder.* I just didn't think you'd be so eager to go back there now that harvest is over."

Realizing he'd been short with Hannes because he was anxious about talking to Susannah's grandfather, Peter said, "There's one last thing I need to discuss with Marshall. It's too important to wait."

Hannes clapped him on the shoulder. "Whatever it's about, I'll be praying the discussion goes smoothly."

That's another gut *change in Hannes's attitude this*

last year, Peter thought. And for that reason, he gladly would have agreed to work on Marshall's farm for *five* harvest seasons…provided he didn't have to give up his courtship with Susannah.

Thankfully, when he got to the farm, he spied Marshall pacing very slowly in front of the barn, and the boys and Lydia were nowhere in sight. Whether or not the old man was surprised to see him, Peter was too nervous to notice. He greeted him and then launched into the speech he'd practiced several times on the way there.

"As you know, even though we were shorthanded and I had to do all the loading and transporting alone, we finished the harvest yesterday—"

He'd barely begun speaking when Marshall interrupted him. "*Jah.* You've held up your end of our agreement to bring in the crop. *Denki.* The *buwe* will take care of winterizing the equipment and any outstanding cleanup. There was no need for you to return to the *bauerei.*"

Despite Marshall's rare expression of gratitude, Peter understood he was being dismissed. But he wasn't leaving until he asked what he'd come there to ask. "Actually, there is a reason for me to return. I'd like you to consider whether I've been a *gut* steward of your farm and—"

Susannah's grandfather seemed to anticipate what Peter was going to say and he interrupted him again. "You've fulfilled your obligation to bring in the harvest. That was what you agreed to do, plain and simple. You also agreed not to court Susannah and I'm holding you to that, too." He started shuffling toward the house.

Isn't he even going to listen to what I have to say? Knowing this was his only chance to make Marshall reconsider their agreement, Peter was determined to speak his piece. He overtook the farmer within three strides and planted himself in his path. Staring him down, he announced, "I *love* Susannah and I believe she loves me."

Marshall's face didn't register any emotion, but he teetered ever so slightly, then growled, "Get out of my way and off of my property, *suh*."

Defeated, Peter stepped aside. How could anyone be so hardheaded? So hard-*hearted*? Peter's own heart was shattered and it took all of his strength to drag himself back to the hitching post. Before he could untie Pepper's lead, he spotted a buggy approaching. Knowing what he had to do, Peter waited for Susannah to stable her horse.

"Hi, Peter," she sang out when she emerged from the barn. "What are you doing here?"

He stammered, "I—I have to tell you something."

"It must be important if you left your workshop in the middle of the day," she said coyly, inching closer to him.

Aware he was about to crush her feelings the way Marshall had crushed his, Peter stiffened his posture and backed away from her. "It *is* important." He licked his lips. "And it's not easy to say. But I—I shouldn't have asked to court you last evening."

The color drained from Susannah's face and her eyes and lips drooped as the gravity of his words settled over her. "You don't want to be my suitor?"

I want to, but I can't, Peter inwardly wailed. Aloud, he apologized, "I'm sorry, Susannah, but *neh*."

"Why not?" Her tone was surprisingly gentle.

Forcing himself, he said, "I don't think we have a

future together." *Only because Marshall won't allow us to have one.*

"But *why* do you think that?" When he didn't answer, she persisted, "Is it that you're worried about your *mamm*'s condition?"

"Her condition?"

"*Jah.* It's my understanding that she may be suffering from depression. But you must know by now that I wouldn't judge anyone for that. And I'd be *hallich* to help her any way I can, for as long as it takes."

Peter shook his head and closed his eyes before opening them again. "This has nothing to do with my *mamm*." Not at this point, it didn't. "I'm sorry, but I have to leave now."

He turned toward his horse, but Susannah grabbed his arm. Her nostrils flared and her cheeks ignited with color once more as she demanded, "If you're breaking up with me because I've gained weight again, then at least be *mann* enough to say the words to my face."

She could have knocked him over with a feather. "What are you talking about? That doesn't even make sense. You're a lot thinner now than you were when I asked to court you last summer." Peter had only meant to point out that she was being illogical, but her features turned as hard as her grandfather's.

In an icy voice, she said, "That just proves how attentive you've been to keeping track of my weight. Don't deny it. You broke up with me out of the blue last *Grischtdaag* when you saw how heavy I'd gotten. And when we embraced last night, you could feel that I'm not that thin. That I've been gaining weight again. You're probably worried I'll gain back every pound I've lost."

Peter was so affronted by her accusation, his voice

rose when he asked her, "Are you kidding me, Susannah? The only person paying that much attention to your weight is *you*."

Thrusting her chin in the air, she challenged, "Okay then, tell me exactly why you don't think we're a *gut* match or why we don't have a future together."

Peter was tempted to say "Because your *groossdaadi* is as wrong about me as you are, that's why." But he couldn't; he'd given him his word. Besides, it wouldn't be worth it. If Susannah truly believed he was the kind of man who valued her appearance over her heart, then maybe they *weren't* a good match for each other. And to think, less than five minutes ago, he'd claimed they loved each other. He looked at the ground and shook his head in disappointment and frustration.

"I knew it," Susannah uttered with disgust when he remained silent. "You showed me your true colors when you broke off our courtship after *Grischtdaag*. I should have paid attention to what you were like the first time."

"Well, if *you* had shown me *your* true colors the first time we courted, I never would have asked you a second time!" Peter countered. Then he got into his buggy and left the farm so quickly a cloud of dust rose in his wake.

"Are you ill?" Lydia had asked after the lunch dishes were done and Susannah announced she needed to go take a nap.

"*Neh.* I'm just tired. Those last three days of picking potatoes without Benuel on the crew wore me out. I'll be fine once I've had some rest," she claimed, heading down the hall.

Susannah had managed to keep herself from crying during their meal, but she couldn't hold back her tears for one more second. She closed her bedroom door and flung herself facedown on the bed, crying into her pillow as she relived the conversation she'd had with Peter near the barn.

How could I have been so naive as to think he truly liked me, inside and out? she lamented. *I should have been* schmaert *enough to learn my lesson the first time.* Not to mention, her grandfather had tried to warn her not to consider Peter as a suitor. Instead, she'd listened to Dorcas and Lydia. She had believed what she'd wanted to believe: namely, that Peter was as smitten with her as she was with him.

No. Not just smitten—that was too frivolous of a word. Susannah had wanted to believe that they were… falling in *love*. She wanted to believe that one day they'd commit their lives to each other. *Ha! He wasn't even my suitor again for one full day before calling off our courtship.* Susannah supposed she should have felt relieved that he'd changed his mind so quickly. At least this way she hadn't had time to get her hopes up even higher before dashing them with the words *I don't think we have a future together.*

How could he do something like that—*twice*—and then have the gall to act as if *she* was the one who was lacking character? It was all so hurtful and confusing and devastating that Susannah wept so hard her head ached. But even then, she didn't stop crying until she finally fell asleep.

For the rest of the day and on Friday, too, she withdrew to her room as frequently as she could, only coming out to make and serve meals or to do her other chores. Sometimes she spent her time alone napping, or in prayer. But most often she simply sat on the edge of her bed and stared out the window, with tears trickling down her face.

On Saturday morning, Marshall said he felt good enough to take the boys to the bus station, since they were returning to Ohio. After packing them a lunch and bidding them goodbye, Susannah slipped away to her room. She had just sat down on the bed when Lydia knocked.

"I'm resting," Susannah called.

Lydia entered, anyway. "Did you say *kumme* in?"

"*Neh.* I said I'm about to lie down. I didn't get much sleep last night." It was true; she'd been awake until almost three thirty…possibly because she'd spent too much time napping on Friday.

"Wouldn't you rather have a cup of *kaffi* with me, now that all the *menner* are out of the *haus*? Or we could take a walk—I noticed you haven't been getting as much fresh air lately."

"*Denki,* but I can hardly keep my eyes open."

"*Jah.* They look a little swollen," Lydia hinted and Susannah knew her stepgrandmother was aware she'd been crying.

But she just said, "I'm fine. Is there anything I can help you with before I take a short snooze?"

"*Neh.* I've got to start doing more things for myself since you'll be leaving us on *Dinnschdaag.*" Lydia frowned. "We'll be sorry to see you go…and not just because of all the work you've done for us."

Susannah gave her a weak smile. "I'll miss you and *Groossdaadi* a lot, too." *But I'll be relieved to leave New Hope so I won't have to worry about running into Peter*, she thought, just like she had when she first arrived in Maine. Then she remembered tomorrow was a church Sunday, meaning the district would gather for worship in the church building. Her stomach knotted up at the thought of seeing Peter, so when Lydia left the room, Susannah decided rather than napping, she needed to pray.

Thankfully, the next day Marshall suggested they sit on a bench in the very back of the gathering room so he could stand against the wall if his back became sore. Susannah couldn't see anyone except the row of people immediately in front of her and Peter wasn't among them. And once the sermons began, she forgot about everything except what the minister was saying. When it came time to prepare and serve lunch, she made a point of staying in the kitchen to set up trays, instead of delivering them to the men upstairs.

When it was the women's turn to eat, Lydia told her they needed to finish their lunch quickly. Marshall was concerned about having back spasms and he was in a hurry to return home, which was more than fine with Susannah.

A few minutes later, she and her stepgrandmother were almost out the door when they bumped into Dorcas, who appeared positively glowing. "Oh, there you are, Susannah. I've been waiting for you. Some of us are going on a hike in the gorge. Do you want to join us?"

Susannah didn't feel like socializing; besides, she didn't know who else was going on the hike. For all she knew, Peter would be there, since he loved the area as much as she did. "I can't… I'm really tired."

"You should go," Lydia urged her. "This is one of your last chances to see your friends."

"*Neh*. But maybe you could *kumme* over for lunch tomorrow?"

"Sure. I'll bring a low-fat dessert," Dorcas offered.

Before they parted, Susannah whispered, "You look *wunderbaar*, Dorcas. Did you lose more weight?"

"Not a pound," she whispered back. "It's because I gained a suitor."

Susannah was genuinely happy for her, since she knew Dorcas wanted to be in a courtship. But all the way home she was troubled with misgivings toward Peter and as soon as she walked into the house, she told her grandparents she was going to her room for a nap.

"Wouldn't you like to do a jigsaw puzzle instead?" Marshall asked.

Susannah was surprised; her grandfather had never initiated a recreational activity, although he often participated when he was invited. Still, she felt too weepy to be around anyone right now. "*Denki*, but I need to rest."

"At least take a walk with me around the yard first. My back is tight and I might need to hold on to you for balance. Lydia's too unsteady to help me."

So they slowly ambled down the lane toward the mailbox. On their way, Marshall cleared his throat. "Lydia and I are concerned about you. Is something wrong?" he asked.

At first she was going to deny it, but she was so moved by her grandfather's open display of concern that she blurted out, "You were right to have reservations about Peter, *Groossdaadi*." Then she confided about their courtship and the reason he'd called it off twice. Finally, she admitted, "I'm sorry I got angry with you for trying to protect me. I should have listened to you."

By then, they'd reached the end of the lane and Marshall grasped the split-rail fence with both hands. Red-faced, he bent forward to stretch his back. "You're right, I was trying to protect you." He sounded short of breath. "You remind me of your *mamm*. I wanted *Gott*'s best for her."

Susannah understood the connection. "*Mamm* and *Daed* may have had their struggles, *Groossdaadi*, but they were *hallich*. They felt blessed."

"*Jah*. Your *daed* is a *gut mann*." Marshall stood up straight again. "Peter Lambright is, too. They both have a lot more character than I do."

Susannah felt stung. "How can you say that after what I just told you?"

"Because the reason Peter ended your courtship had nothing to do with you. He ended it because *I* told him he had to."

Susannah couldn't believe what she was hearing as her grandfather described the agreement he'd made with Peter and the conversation that he'd had on Thursday. She felt so hurt and angry and betrayed she could hardly look at her grandfather.

"How could you do something like that to Peter? And to *me*?" she cried.

"I thought I was doing it for your *gut*," he said. "But when I saw how miserable you've been and when I reconsidered Peter's character, I realized I was wrong. I'm sorry, Susannah, and I hope you'll forgive me."

Susannah hesitated before nodding. "*Jah*, I forgive you, *Groossdaadi*," she said. *I just hope Peter forgives* me.

"I'm going to take a walk over to the workshop and back," Peter told his mother as he lifted his coat from a hook near the door.

"Maybe you ought to take a nap instead," she urged him. "Not that I'm anyone to point a finger, but you've seemed more tired these past few days than you did when you were working two jobs."

Peter hadn't been tired—he'd been miserable. Dejected. Heartsick. So taking a nap wasn't going to help. Taking a walk probably wouldn't help him, either, but at least it would get him out of the house. He didn't want his cheerless mood to bring down his mother, especially now that she felt so hopeful again.

The nutritionist she'd consulted last week had suggested Dorothy get additional lab work done. When the results came back on Friday, they indicated she had a form of anemia that was severe, but manageable. Part of her health plan included receiving vitamin B-12 injections. Just knowing that she would receive effective treatment helped boost her spirit even before it was administered.

"Who would ever think I'd look forward to receiving an injection?" she had said, marveling after hearing the news. Although it was a doctor who had made the diagnosis, Dorothy credited the nutritionist for suggesting the lab work in the first place. And she said she never would have gone to a nutritionist if it hadn't been for her conversation with Susannah.

She was so grateful that on Saturday afternoon she'd baked a pie with the last of the blueberries Eva had frozen from the summer harvest. Dorothy intended to personally deliver it to the farm, so she could share her good news with Susannah. As Peter was leaving the house, she reminded him, "Eva and I won't leave for another hour. If you change your mind, you're *wilkom* to *kumme* with us."

"I won't change my mind," Peter replied, knowing that neither Susannah nor Marshall would welcome him on the farm. Nor did he want to see them. In time, he'd get over his hurt, but right now, he was still praying about it. And since he could pray as he walked, he meandered on the long road between his house and the workshop for almost an hour. Finally, he decided it was probably time for his mother and sister to leave and he headed into the barn to hitch the horse so they wouldn't have to do it themselves.

Pepper was friskier than usual and he took the time to brush her coat and mane, hoping that would settle her down. His mother had mentioned last week that she'd had difficulty handling him. *It's too bad Hannes isn't home or he could bring Mamm and Eva to the farm,* he thought.

At that very moment, he heard Hannes's buggy approaching, so he led Pepper back into his stall. When he came out, he was dumbfounded to see Susannah standing in the doorway. "Hi, Peter." She tentatively moved closer. "May I speak with you a minute?"

Speechless, he nodded. Although he didn't have anything else to say, he could at least listen to her.

"My—my *groossdaadi* told me about the loan," she began.

Peter immediately saw red. *How dare Marshall not hold up his end of the bargain after harping on me to hold up mine. Is he really that vengeful? Or was he trying to make me look bad as a way of ensuring Susannah would never accept me as a suitor?* If that was the case, he needn't have bothered; Peter didn't have any interest whatsoever in courting her now.

"He shouldn't have told you—he broke his word.

Our arrangement is none of your business and I don't want to talk about it. You'll have to excuse me. I'm going inside." He started toward the door but Susannah blocked his path.

"Please, just listen to me," she pleaded, her voice quavering. So Peter stood still, allowing her to continue. "He only told me about it because he regrets how he treated you. He knows how much character you have. So do I, and I'm sorry for implying you were superficial. You were right—I was the only one who was focused on my weight. But that was just because I couldn't figure out what else had changed to make you break up with me…" Susannah covered her face with her hands and dissolved into tears.

So Peter took her by the shoulders and directed her toward a hay bale, where they sat down side by side, just like they used to do at lunchtime. "I can only imagine how confusing and frustrating it must have been for you not to know the real reason. I hope you'll forgive me for not being more honest from the beginning."

"Of course I forgive you. It wasn't your fault that you couldn't tell me—that was part of your arrangement with *Groossdaadi.*"

"*Neh*, that's not what I mean." Peter looked at his boots, unable to meet her eyes as he told her about Hannes wrecking the SUV and the *Englischers* demanding immediate reimbursement for the damage. He concluded by acknowledging, "I was trying to protect my *bruder* and my *mamm*, but I should have been more honest about why I needed a loan in the first place. I should have trusted the Lord to provide a way to help my *familye* without hurting you. Without *losing* you…"

Susannah nudged his shoulder with hers. "You haven't lost me—I'm right here."

Peter swiveled his head to see if she was serious. "You'd accept me as your suitor a third time?"

"*Jah.* I would—and I do."

Epilogue

"Have you seen my husband?" Susannah asked, surveying the crowded gathering room in the church. She and Peter had been married earlier in the day and the guests were enjoying supper and dessert, but Peter was nowhere to be found. "He said he had to do something outside, but he's been gone a while."

"*Neh*, I haven't," Lydia replied as Honor Bawell approached them, carefully balancing a plate of desserts.

"I can't believe you decided to have peanut-butter pies for your *hochzich*," Honor remarked.

Although a small number of Amish brides served large, bakery-made cakes similar to what might be found at an *Englischer* wedding, most did not. Instead, the Amish made their wedding cakes, as well as an assortment of desserts. Peanut-butter pie may have been included as one of the treats, but it wasn't usually the main offering, as it was at Peter and Susannah's wedding.

"It's my favorite," Susannah said. "Especially the way Lydia makes it."

After Honor walked away, Lydia asked, "Have you tasted it yet?"

"*Jah.* It's as *appenditlich* as ever. I was considering having another small slice," Susannah said. "*Denki* for making them. And for everything else you did to prepare for our *hochzich.*"

"It wasn't difficult—I had a lot of help from Charity, Dorcas, Eva and Dorothy."

Throughout the course of her treatment during the past year, Peter's mother had increasingly experienced improvements in her health and mood. Now she claimed she had even more energy than she'd had before becoming anemic. Likewise, Lydia's wrist was completely mended—although she referred to it as her internal weather vane, because she felt mild pain whenever there was a storm coming.

"I have something to confess," Lydia whispered. "We used a lower-sugar, lower-fat recipe."

"I couldn't taste any difference," Susannah marveled. "But now I'm *definitely* going to have a second piece."

She went to the dessert table and took slices of pie for both her and Peter. *Where is he?* she wondered, scanning the room. She had endured being separated from him during their one-year long-distance courtship, but she didn't want to be separated from him on her wedding day, too. When she didn't see him anywhere among the guests, she edged toward the door and slipped out into the cool November evening. It was too dark for her to see very far and she was about to turn around and go back inside when Hannes came toward her.

"Are you looking for Peter?" he asked, and when she

said she was, he led her to where Peter was standing beside a buggy wagon near the hitching rail.

"What are you doing out here?" she asked Peter as Hannes walked away. "And why is this wagon here? You arrived in your buggy, didn't you?"

Peter chuckled. "*Jah.* Hannes brought this here for me. *Kumme,* I want to show you something." He took the two plates from her hand and set them inside the wagon. Then he climbed up and held out his arms to assist her into it, too.

Handing her a flashlight, Peter told Susannah to point it toward the bed of the wagon. She turned it on, illuminating an octagonal picnic table with separate benches, similar to the one he'd made for the *Englischers'* wedding last year. "I made this for you— for *us.* But I rounded the corners on the tabletop and the benches, so our *kinner* won't get hurt if they bump into the ends."

The words *our kinner* took Susannah's breath away. She couldn't wait to start a family with Peter. "*Denki.* It's *wunderbaar,*" she said. Then she teased flirtatiously, "I notice you didn't engrave our initials and *hochzich* day on the table like the *Englischers* did."

"*Neh.* That would be superficial, when *Gott* wants us to look beneath the surface." Peter grinned as she crouched down. Pointing, he told her to shine the flashlight at the underside of the table. Susannah bent down beside him and aimed the beam of light where he'd indicated. She had to tilt her head to see it: Peter had inscribed their full names and today's date in the center of the table. Springing up, she clapped her hands together.

"I love it," she murmured. Clicking off the flashlight, she drew nearer to him.

"And I love *you*." Peter gently lifted her prayer *kapp* strings and placed them behind her shoulders. Cupping her face in his strong, calloused hands, he leaned down and kissed her until she was dizzy. She faltered as she pulled away, but Peter slid his hands to her waist and steadied her.

Relishing his touch, Susannah inched closer. "I have an idea. Let's eat our pie at our new table."

So they sat side by side in the near-dark atop of the buggy wagon, eating their dessert very, very slowly. And even after it was gone, the newlyweds lingered there a while longer. Because as Lydia had once told them, sweet things were meant to be savored.

* * * * *

If you enjoyed this story by Carrie Lighte,
be sure to pick up the first book in
The Amish of New Hope miniseries,
Hiding Her Amish Secret.

Available now from Love Inspired!

And look for more Amish romances every month
from Love Inspired!

Dear Reader,

During a recent trip to Lancaster County, my mother received a coupon to a local market for a free whoopie pie because it was her birthday. The sweet treat was about the size of a salad plate and we divided it among the five of us who were traveling together. In that same market, we also purchased a butternut squash grown on a local Amish farm. Both the dessert and the veggie were so fresh and delicious that I've searched high and low to find something of similar quality in my community. So far, nothing I've tasted compares to the whoopie pie and squash we had that day. But I'll keep looking—either that, or I'll have to return to Lancaster again soon.

I completed this book right around the first of the year. One my resolutions for 2021 is to practice better eating habits and to get more exercise. (Not an easy feat when I'm sitting down and writing about traditional Amish cooking; my mouth starts to water after two sentences! Again, I'll persevere…)

Whatever you're eating for supper tonight, I hope you enjoy it in good health.

Blessings,
Carrie Lighte